D1618811

the Reaper of Zons

A Zons CRIME NOVEL

Also by Catherine Shepherd

Zons Crime series

Fatal Puzzle

the Reaper of Zons

A Zons CRIME NOVEL

CATHERINE SHEPHERD

Translated by Julia A. Knobloch

amazon crossing

This is a work of fiction. Names, characters, organizations, places, events, and incidents are either products of the author's imagination or are used fictitiously.

Text copyright © 2013 Catherine Shepherd
Translation copyright © 2016 Julia A. Knobloch

All rights reserved.

No part of this book may be reproduced, or stored in a retrieval system, or transmitted in any form or by any means, electronic, mechanical, photocopying, recording, or otherwise, without express written permission of the publisher.

Previously published as *Der Sichelmörder von Zons* by the author via the Kindle Direct Publishing Platform in Germany in 2013. Translated from German by Julia Knobloch. First published in English by AmazonCrossing in 2016.

Published by AmazonCrossing, Seattle

www.apub.com

Amazon, the Amazon logo, and AmazonCrossing are trademarks of Amazon.com, Inc., or its affiliates.

ISBN-13: 9781503952980
ISBN-10: 1503952983

Cover design by Edward Bettison

Printed in the United States of America

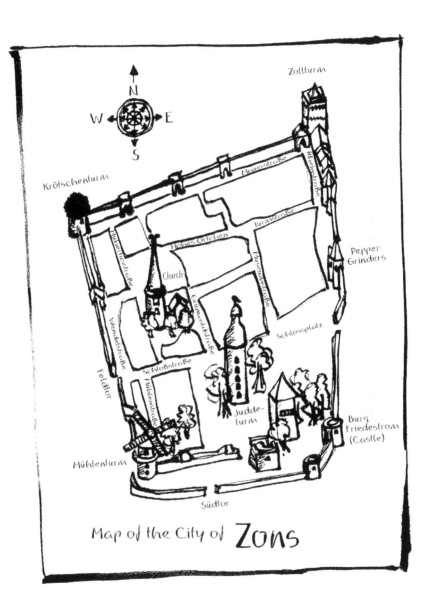

Map of the City of Zons

I

Five Hundred Years Ago

The sails of the mill were buzzing in the wind. Many months had passed since Bastian had rescued Marie from the dungeon. Now he was idling in a meadow in the sunshine and chewing on a blade of grass. He was very pleased with himself. They may not have arrested the killer Dietrich Hellenbroich, but they had thwarted his megalo-maniacal master plan and prevented more killings in Zons. Bastian was leaning back on his elbows and squinting up at the hot summer sun when he suddenly heard a loud roaring sound nearby. He sat up and looked in the direction of the noise. Then he glanced over at the city wall and froze.

Bastian couldn't believe his eyes. One of the fortified watchtow-ers had collapsed almost entirely, and heavy stones were tumbling down the slope toward the Rhine meadows. The tower had split in two along most of its length. There was hardly anything left of one side of it, and Bastian could see more stones and mortar raining down from the portion that remained. Suddenly, he felt the ground trembling underneath him. The movement seemed to come from the foot of the watchtower. The tremors spread out fast and grew stronger. The soil heaved up and down, creaking and groaning, until eventually Bastian's body vibrated, too. The groaning grew louder and louder until the immense tension was too much for the Earth's crust, and the ground next to Bastian caved in. For a moment, the dust that blew up from the ground covered the sun. Then, just as abruptly, everything fell silent.

What was going on? Bastian's eyes and mouth were dry from the dust-filled air, making it difficult to see or breathe. He coughed so hard it felt as if his chest was going to explode, and he spit out the dust, his throat raw. He kneeled on the broken earth and propped up his body with his hands, trying to compose himself. After spitting out more dust, he wiped his face. His eyes watered. He tried to focus on something, but the world around him was blurry, as if wrapped in a milky veil. A myriad of fine dust particles kept pricking at his eyes, causing an endless stream of burning tears.

When the air had cleared enough for Bastian to discern at least the outline of his surroundings, he noticed a long, straight trench at his feet. No more than twenty inches wide, it resembled a trail. Sand trickled down from the edges. As the dusty fog lifted, Bastian's breathing relaxed. He stared at the trench.

Was it an earthquake? What else could have caused the earth to collapse in on itself like that? Then again, it was quite different from earthquakes he'd experienced before. This time, the vibrations were smaller but the earth in front of him had sunk quite a bit more. He cautiously stood and looked around. The sun was shining, and the birds on the branches of the tree above him had resumed their tweeting. Insects buzzed through the air, and a cluster of small black bugs landed on his sweat-soaked skin. Bastian swatted at his arms, hoping to chase away the bugs. He shook his disheveled blond hair, which caused another dust storm.

Well, he thought, *if it wasn't an earthquake, what was it?*

He reached for a long, knobby branch he had spotted under the tree and poked the edge of the trench with it. The earth didn't move.

Then he shifted his weight and carefully stepped down. The ground seemed solid. Gathering courage, he stepped in with his other leg. Now he was standing smack in the middle of the trench—and the earth had not swallowed him. He hopped up and down a few times, testing whether it was really safe. The ground was as stable as if the trench had been there forever.

.   .   .

He was freezing. Bitterly freezing, despite the summer heat. He heard water dripping. Thousands of tiny drops were trickling down from the vaulted ceiling and the rough stone walls, which echoed his rattling breath. It almost sounded as if his breathing itself were screaming for help. Almost—for he no longer had a tongue to scream with. All that was left of his tongue was a big, swollen, bloodshot knot in his throat that tasted like metal and threatened to choke him.

Initially, he had tried to free himself. But the nails that stuck out everywhere from the chair he was fettered to only bore deeper into his flesh, causing hellish pain at the slightest movement. He resigned himself to keeping as still as possible in the cold darkness. He had lost all sense of time. His chattering thoughts spun from hope to horror and back, searching frantically for a loophole through which to escape from this nightmare. Yet he always came to the same realization: he would not leave this dark, cold, damp hole alive. A scream-like sound broke from his swollen throat. Tears ran down his cheeks. Nobody could hear him.

And so he remained alone down there, the pain and terror his sole, unmerciful companions—waiting for his tormentor to reappear from the shadows.

.   .   .

Bastian advanced, one cautious step at a time. *How could a trench this size appear so suddenly?* He held a hand to his forehead to shade his eyes from the gleaming sunlight. He squinted, his brown eyes narrowing to thin slits as he gauged the length of the trench. It had to be at least one hundred yards away from the watchtower that had collapsed.

A small crowd had gathered at the foot of the tower. Even from a distance, Bastian could hear the astonished murmur of the people. He thought it strange that they would gather there, of all places. The tremors had been so violent that many of the houses in Zons must have collapsed as well. After all, the watchtower had been built with huge stones, whereas many of the tiny houses were made of weaker materials—surely a result of the townspeople's poverty. During the earthquake three years ago, five houses had collapsed. He remembered vividly the many aftershocks and how the ground had trembled for minutes on end before the silence settled in. Everyone had been afraid to go back into their homes, so the townspeople had spent the night outside, in huts hastily erected from hay, or under the sky, despite the chilly winter night.

Now he gave the trench another look and began to walk faster. The ground felt solid and hard under his feet. Perhaps this was not the result of an earthquake. The trench was unnaturally straight until it stopped with a sharp edge about twenty yards from the crumbled watchtower. None of the people inspecting the ruins paid any attention to the trench. They stood with their backs to Bastian, craning their necks to stare at the heaps of stones.

Bastian recognized his best friend, Wernhart, who was, like Bastian, a member of the City Guard. Wernhart stood next to Josef Hesemann, the town doctor, another of Bastian's close friends. A few months ago, Bastian and Wernhart had spent several chilly winter nights together chasing a serial killer who played at a fatal puzzle, with local townspeople as his pawns. Although Bastian was younger than Wernhart and hadn't been with the City Guard as long, he had quickly moved up the ranks and was responsible for keeping Zons safe from all sorts of thieves and murderers. He owed his career to Father Johannes, the local priest, who had taught him at an early age how to read and write, despite Bastian being only the youngest son of the Zons miller. The priest had educated and raised Bastian to be the righteous young man he was today. Tall and sinewy, Bastian would clearly have made an excellent miller, but that position had been given to his oldest brother, Heinrich, who now provided Zons and the surrounding area with his finely ground flour.

"Wernhart!" Bastian yelled into the crowd. "What happened?"

Wernhart turned around in surprise. His blue eyes flashed when he recognized Bastian.

"Come see for yourself. The tower collapsed!"

"Are any other buildings damaged?"

"No. Apart from the tower, every brick seems to be in place. Even the shingles on old Jacob's rooftop haven't moved an inch."

Jacob's was arguably the most humble house in Zons. Because the family couldn't afford repairs after the last earthquake, they had reroofed the house with chunks of wood and hay, and the roof looked like a patchwork quilt.

The people were still staring at the damaged watchtower. Apparently, they hadn't even noticed the mysterious line of sunken earth behind them.

II
Present

Oliver's heart was racing like crazy. He held a beautiful bouquet of long-stemmed, dark-red roses and nervously licked his dry lips as he waited. Would Emily show up? The last time, he had been very late for their date, which had ruined the entire evening. Oliver sensed that Emily's disappointment had made her withdraw. And under no circumstances did he want her to distance herself from him. Not now. Not when he had finally managed to get closer to her.

That's why he had thought of something romantic for their Sunday afternoon. At least, he believed most women would find it romantic. He had asked Emily to meet him in Neuss's city park, under the big old chestnut tree at the edge of the green where they had kissed for the first time. A shiver ran down his spine as he recalled the first taste of her soft, full lips. As their initial, tentative exchange had grown into a deep and passionate kiss, Oliver had been aroused by a desire unlike any he had ever known. However, as intense as Emily's passion had been, so was her wrath on their last date when Oliver had stood her up for two hours because his boss wouldn't let him off.

Hans Steuermark, the chief inspector of the Crime Division for the Rhine–County Neuss, was well known for his tenacity. Solving the case was the top priority. And what was true for the boss therefore had to hold true for his employees, too. As the last hire on the squad, Oliver knew that all too well.

Today Oliver wanted to make up for last time. He had spread a large blanket under the chestnut tree and placed a dark-brown wicker picnic basket in the shadow cast by the tree's mighty crown. The cork of the champagne bottle peeked out on one side of the basket. Everything was perfect. Only Emily was missing.

Oliver looked anxiously at his watch. She was already ten minutes late. Maybe she'd be coming from another direction? Just as he was about to turn around, he spotted her petite silhouette out of the corner of his eye.

Oliver was unable to utter even a simple hello and just grinned at her, thoroughly enchanted. Fortunately, she didn't seem to notice his nervousness. With small, steady steps, she quickly walked up to him, stood on her tiptoes, wrapped one arm around his neck, and planted a sweet kiss on his cheek.

"I'm sorry. Traffic was terrible," she whispered.

Although Oliver was speechless, his body reacted. He flung his arms around her slender waist and drew her closer. He looked her deep in the eyes and kissed her.

. . .

Twelve miles away, in the Rhine meadows near Zons, another couple was spending the beautiful summer day on a romantic date. Nina and Tobias were cuddling and kissing on a picnic blanket. High grasses hid them from the glances of passersby strolling a nearby path, taking in the view of the Rhine. Only a few dogs, in pursuit of an interesting scent, disturbed the two lovers. But when Tobias rolled on top of Nina, she let out a loud yelp, pushed him away, and sat up. Her face was contorted with pain, and she rubbed her back.

"What happened?" Tobias asked.

"No idea. Something really sharp just dug into my back."

Tobias checked the soft blanket and felt something poking up from underneath. He pushed the blanket aside and grabbed for the object. He didn't recognize what he was looking at, as it was firmly stuck in the ground. He dug around it until its hold gradually loosened. At first, it looked like part of an old branch that had been stripped of its bark. Tobias kept pulling until he held the object in his hand.

"Ew, gross, what is that?" Nina said, recoiling.

"I don't know. But don't worry; it won't bite." Tobias grinned and dangled the mysterious object in front of Nina. "Nothing to be scared of! It's just a bone. I bet one of the dogs buried it here."

The find consisted of several pieces of bone that were all linked together. Tobias was just about to hurl them into the Rhine when Nina grabbed his arm and took the bones out of his hand.

"These aren't animal bones," she said.

Nina frowned and took a closer look. Something about the bones seemed familiar. A first-year medical-school student at Heinrich Heine University in Düsseldorf, she had just successfully completed her anatomy exam. She had found the subject fascinating, despite the exhausting challenge of remembering the more than two hundred bones of the human skeleton and their abstruse Latin names.

She ran her fingers over the bone. On one end it was rounded, which made her think it must be part of a heel. Firmly attached to it were other bones; she put a fingertip on the cuboid, recalling its Latin name: *os cuboideum.* Then followed the two outer metatarsal bones, the *ossa metatarsalia.* On these smallest and second-smallest toes, segments were missing—the middle phalanx and distal phalanx. Almost nothing was left of the other toes; their metatarsals and phalanges were gone. Judging from the size of the bone, it had probably belonged to a male foot—Nina estimated it to be size 9. Tobias wore the same shoe size. The thought scared her, and she dropped the bones.

"These are human bones, Tobias. What should we do?"

Tobias scratched his head and thought for a moment. The bones looked old. It didn't seem likely that they were the remains of a person who had recently died—or been murdered. Yellowed as they were, they must have been buried centuries ago. He picked up the bones. One end of the foot bone was slightly supple, which struck Tobias as odd, since he had always imagined that bones grew drier over time until they finally became porous and fell to dust. Yet this one was pliable, at least on one end.

"Let's go to the police," he said as he stood and offered Nina his outstretched hand.

.   .   .

Anna shook her head and scowled. She really hated the monthly Monday meetings, when the staff received their new targets. This time, her boss had come up with something particularly fancy. In just a couple of weeks she was supposed to sell a new kind of yen swap, and, to make things worse, this product wasn't suited for any of her current clients. She ran her finger over the list of names the bank had identified as target customers—members with a certain minimum balance. Anna had a narrow window to find buyers for those ten million euros; the matter was pressing, because the bank needed to offset some of its recent risk-weighted positions—increasingly complicated products invented so the bank could continue bringing in profit.

Many of Anna's regular clients belonged to the German middle class and had made considerable profits over the years, thanks to Anna's counsel. In the few cases where the speculation hadn't yielded positive results, she'd always tried her best to find ways for the investor to even out the losses. Obviously, this didn't always work out, but her clients were generally satisfied with Anna's advice. Still, this new product appeared to be highly speculative. After the nuclear disaster in Fukushima, who would bid on the soaring yen? How was she supposed to convince even a single client that this was a worthwhile investment?

As she brooded over the list of names, Anna ran her fingers through her long, curly hair—a habit ever since she was a little girl, calming herself whenever she felt uncertain. Anna was a banker through and through. But she was not motivated only by financial theory—she needed to make enough money so she could finally have her dream garden. She loved flowers and wanted to plant them on her very own property someday. Ever since last year, when she had barely escaped the hands of a serial killer, the mastermind behind what the press had coined a "fatal puzzle," she was even more committed to her goal. If she received a large-enough bonus this year, she might be able to afford to buy a condo with a large backyard. But how could she get there?

Suddenly, the memory of Bastian Mühlenberg, a detective who had lived five hundred years ago, flashed in her mind. Anna had no rational explanation for these weird apparitions, but she was certain that the man had somehow traversed time and space. Emily, her best friend, thought she was just imagining things because of the tremendous psychological stress she had been under. But Anna knew she had met Bastian for real. Though she hadn't seen him again since that evening when he had wanted to meet her at the so-called *Mühlenturm*, the Miller's Tower, in Zons. She missed him—or, rather, what could have become of them under different circumstances.

The shrill sound of her phone ringing made her jump.

"Sweetie, what's up?" Jimmy's voice was deep and seductive. "Just spoke with Tom. I understand you guys are supposed to sell the new yen swaps?"

"Yeah. I bet your department screwed up again and now we have to make up for it."

"Now, now, honey. Relax. I've got some interesting info for you. How about lunch, today or tomorrow?"

Anna rolled her eyes. That was *so* like him, always chasing the next adventure. On the other hand, Jimmy had helped her out before. He was so well connected that he might be able to recommend someone who could actually benefit from that new swap.

III
Five Hundred Years Ago

An eternity must have passed. The water continued to drip down the vault's massive walls. Outside, summer was in full swing, but down here it was uncomfortably cold and damp. He shivered. He hoped his torturer had forgotten about him and that he would eventually pass out from thirst and exhaustion and sink gently into the redeeming arms of death.

Then, suddenly, barely recognizable against the dark stone wall, a silhouette approached him at a measured pace. The figure manifested itself as a huge shadow. How long had his torturer been watching him?

The shadow whispered hoarsely: *"Non loqueris contra proximum tuum falsum testimonium."* At the same moment, a crop cut through the darkness with a buzzing sound and struck his shivering skin. He remembered that sentence. It was from the Bible. It was the eighth commandment: *You shall not give false testimony against your neighbor.*

His hand clad in a hard leather glove, the shadow brutally grabbed the man's chin. All he could see was a black face framed by a dark hood.

"I ordered you to repent! Yet you kept on sinning, with no regard for your master's wishes!"

The prisoner desperately tried to shake his head. No. That was not true. He had not sinned. Yet the black hand gripped his chin so tightly that moving was impossible, and nothing but a dull sound escaped his throat. He tore at his fetters, and the nails on the chair bored even deeper into his raw flesh. His heart hammered. Sweat drenched his forehead. He stared wide-eyed into the black abyss of the stranger's face and tried to convince the man of his innocence. He had not done anything wrong! He wasn't a liar!

That very second, a memory shot through his brain like an arrow. Indeed, he had lied—not terrible lies, though. And he had not repented! In that sense, he realized, the shadow was right. He had not repented the way he had been told—but he had paid for his sins. The letter of indulgence was hidden under his pillow. This man had no right to punish him; he had behaved correctly.

The shadow figure's eerie mouth came close to his ear. "You did not repent for your sins as I commanded. Now the Lord makes you repent through my hand, as He has chosen me to enforce what He commands."

The vile presence moved away from him. Suddenly, a flickering candle illuminated the vault. The prisoner closed his eyes from the sudden brightness.

"Look at me!" hissed the dark figure. The prisoner obeyed.

The black-cloaked man held a clay vessel in his right hand. With his left hand, he breached the vessel with a sharpened wooden stick and produced a wobbly, bloodred piece of flesh.

Ice-cold terror flashed through the prisoner's veins when he recognized that it was a tongue. The shadow nodded and smirked.

"Oh, yes, sinner. This is your liar's tongue. I preserved it so it shall speak forever of your sins while you burn in hell!"

The shackled man shook his head in panic. His flesh hurt, but fear had him so firmly in its grip, he hardly felt any pain. All his attention was directed at the man in the black cloak holding the sheared-off tongue. His thoughts returned once more to the letter of indulgence under his pillow. As if reading his mind, the dark figure thundered, "Do you really think you can pay your way to redemption? Don't you know that, in order to achieve atonement, your confession must be thorough and your heart filled with regret? And you are required to do good deeds!"

The shadow placed the jug with the tongue on the floor and once again loomed above his victim. He grabbed the man's hair and yanked his head back, exposing his unprotected throat.

"You shall simmer in hell eternally because I have preserved your tongue. And now, sinner, your time to die has come!"

With these words, the dark figure pulled a golden sickle from under his cloak and, with one smooth movement, severed his victim's throat. Blood splashed from the man's carotid in a high fountain and everything went dark, but one last thought rushed through his brain: *My name is Conrad, and I am not a sinner.*

. . .

Bastian and Wernhart were sitting with their jars of mead in Zons's tiny Old Hen Tavern. Sizzling meat roasted over an open fire. The delicious smell filled every corner of the cramped space and made Bastian's mouth water. He could barely wait to sink his teeth into the savory roast and take a hearty bite.

A couple of hours earlier, he and Wernhart had walked the entire town—and, with the exception of the huge watchtower, which had collapsed like a house of cards before his very eyes, Bastian could confirm that no other buildings had been damaged.

Bastian enjoyed a large gulp of mead and glanced over to the fire. A sudden draft caused the flames to flare up, and Bastian turned his attention toward the door. Josef Hesemann, the doctor, stood searching the nooks and crannies of the tiny room. When he spotted Bastian, he approached the table.

"Greetings! I'm looking for Conrad. Have you seen him?"

"No, but sit with us!"

Josef nodded and grabbed a seat. His cousin Conrad was a monk in nearby Knechtsteden Abbey. He was a regular visitor in Josef's house, where he helped by caring for and comforting the sick.

"Here you go. Enjoy!" The tavern keeper set a heavy wooden board on the rough tabletop. The platter was laden with crisp brown pieces of meat. Wasting no time, the three friends lunged for the food.

After they had devoured the meal, Josef said, "I was supposed to meet Conrad an hour ago, but I don't remember whether we were meeting at my place or here at the tavern."

Bastian had opened his mouth to answer, when another blast of air swept through the room. Wrapped in eerie silence, seven members of the Fraternity of Saint Sebastian walked over to a free table, sat down, and leaned into a huddle. A conspiratorial murmur rose above the silence of the room.

"See over there?" whispered Bastian. "The Committee of the Seven Arrows. I wonder what scheme they're hatching this time."

Wernhart and Josef inconspicuously turned their heads toward the seven men. Up until a few years ago, the hundred-year-old fraternity had enjoyed an impeccable reputation among the townspeople of Zons. But after the senior master, Henricus Krumbein, had been buried with full honors, and a new master, Huppertz Helpenstein, had assumed leadership, things had changed. Under Henricus, the fraternity members had distinguished themselves through military excellence and courage during the siege of Neuss in 1475, when they fought the occupying army of Emperor Friedrich. But these qualities had waned and given way to an increasingly extremist religious orientation.

Huppertz Helpenstein was a notorious fundamentalist who had introduced a new set of rules for the Fraternity of Saint Sebastian. Now, piousness counted more than strategic skill and military-defense tactics. The Saint Sebastian altar of the local Saint Martin's Church had been built with funds from a generous donation from Huppertz, who insisted on a monthly confession from his brothers, despite the fact that the Fourth Council of the Lateran of 1215 commanded Christians to confess only once per year.

Each of the seven brothers in the tavern was dressed in black garments. Their characteristic tall, pointed felt hats with broad brims sat stacked on a bench beside the table. The men were so absorbed in their conversation, they seemed unaware of the other patrons. The tavern keeper put a jug of wine on their table and quickly disappeared behind his open-fire grill.

Then Huppertz, the oldest of the seven men, raised his hand and pointed at one of the brothers sitting on the opposite side of the table. The man bowed and with one hand reached for his neck. For a moment, Bastian caught sight of a delicate silver necklace that was swiftly handed over to Huppertz and vanished inside a pocket of his jerkin.

"Did you see that?" Bastian asked.

"Yes, it looked like there was a small key hanging from the chain," whispered Wernhart. "It is said that only three keys at once can open the fraternity's sacred chest. My father once told me that there are two keys in the fraternity's possession, and the local priest keeps the third. Apparently, the chest holds secret writings and valuable treasures."

Bastian cringed. He had not averted his eyes from the fraternity's table; Huppertz must have sensed Bastian's intense gaze, and he turned and skewered Bastian with a piercing look. But Bastian didn't blink. The eerie, silent competition lasted for several moments. Then Huppertz nodded and turned away.

Bastian let out a long exhale. The way Huppertz had stared at him was disconcerting—as if he wanted to glean Bastian's innermost thoughts. In an attempt to chase away the eerie sensation, Bastian shook his head and stood. He was eager to leave and get some distance from the fraternity.

"I promised Marie I wouldn't be long. I'll see you at sunrise, at the watchtower ruins."

Bastian nodded to Josef and headed toward the exit without looking back at the fraternity members. Then he slipped into the darkness.

IV
Present

Detective Oliver Bergmann thoroughly examined the foot bones: two metatarsals with missing upper links. The three larger toes had been severed. Oliver flipped through the lab report. It described the cuts as considerably smooth with only a few serrated edges, therefore excluding saws or knives with a coarse cutting blade as potential murder weapons. Oliver chewed his lips and, deep in thought, scratched the back of his head. This case seemed odd.

A few days ago, the young couple who had encountered these bones had called the police. At first, nobody took them seriously. The bones looked very old and tattered. Plus, in Zons and surrounding areas, where quite a few archaeological excavations had taken place, finding old human bones wasn't breaking news. Just recently, during the renovation of the museum courtyard, the remains of a large vault had been discovered. The archaeologists were still trying to determine the age of the vault. Since the courtyard had served as the city's marketplace up until the beginning of the nineteenth century, experts assumed the vault was probably from the seventeenth or eighteenth century—or possibly even much older.

Oliver recalled an article from a few weeks ago. During one of Zons's larger excavations from the 1980s, they had found 261 human skeletons near Burg Friedestrom, the fort. The archaeologists concluded that there had been a surplus of men in medieval Zons. They noticed that only a few skeletons revealed traces of violence and that the life expectancy of the general population had been remarkably high for the era. Despite characteristically bad hygienic conditions, these people had been astonishingly healthy. Even the child mortality rate, at 18 percent, had been far below average.

Oliver smiled. He would never have read those kinds of articles had it not been for Emily. She was the reason he had recently developed an interest in historical works. Ever since they'd met during the investigation of his last big murder case, anything remotely related to her caught his interest—her Italian heritage, her favorite foods, her knowledge of history. He was convinced that without her, the investigation would have dragged on much longer. An extremely talented journalism student at Cologne University, she had become something of a local celebrity when she'd written a feature series for the regional paper, the *Rheinische Post*, about a serial killer who had brutally raped and murdered several women in the fifteenth century—what they had come to call a "fatal puzzle." Thanks to Emily's expertise about those historic murder cases, Oliver and his partner Klaus had managed to solve the puzzle and catch a present-day copycat killer who'd struck terror into the citizens of Zons in a relatively short time.

Oliver turned his attention back to the remains of the human foot that lay wrapped in a plastic bag on the desk. Word of this find had quickly spread around Headquarters. Initially, even Oliver had joked about it. Poor guy. Making out with his girlfriend on a beautiful summer day, only to unearth some ugly old bones. Oliver thought about his picnic with Emily on that same day.

But the lab report had changed things. Now they were dealing with a human foot that had happily walked this Earth as recently as a few weeks ago. What's more, traces of hydrochloric acid had been detected.

Oliver opened the plastic bag. Carefully, he bent one end of the bone up and down. The sensation was disgusting, as if he was playing with a big, wobbly gummy bear. Appalled, Oliver dropped the plastic bag onto his desk and grabbed the lab report again.

The hydrochloric acid had dissolved the solid bone substance, scientifically known as tricalcium phosphate, leaving nothing but collagen. Oliver knew that collagen was a soft, pliable compound that was widely used in the production of gelatin. And gelatin was one of the basic ingredients of . . . gummy bears! Oliver felt queasy.

His office door flew open and slammed against the wall. Klaus stumbled into the room. He barely managed to hold a coffee mug while squeezing a pile of three-ring binders under his arm. The binders were in disarray and threatened to fall to the floor. Klaus tried to steady the binders with his chin and winked at Oliver, mumbling a greeting. With three quick steps he cut through the office to his desk, where he dropped the binders. He was drenched in sweat and plopped into his chair, put his feet up on the desk, and took a long sip of coffee.

"Good morning, buddy. Already busy working on our latest case?"

"Mock me as much as you want, but Steuermark expects us to present him with our game plan in an hour." Oliver smirked, grabbed the plastic bag, and tossed it over to Klaus, who caught the bag and looked at it in disgust.

"Yuck. Are these the bones everyone's talking about? There's hardly anything left! And where are we supposed to find the body that belongs to this foot, if there even is one?"

.   .   .

The only light he saw fell through a tiny crack. The light was so faint it didn't even reach down to the floor. Other than that, darkness surrounded him. The gag in his mouth was unbearably scratchy, and a relentless heat filled the tiny cage he was in. It felt well above a hundred degrees. He lay on one side, tied up, his knees pulled close. His hands were bound over his chest, and several ropes were wrapped around his legs. Seen from above, he would have resembled an embryo in the womb.

The oppressive heat and lack of fresh air made him dizzy. He couldn't recall how he had ended up here. The last thing he remembered was a blonde beauty at the networking mixer one of his clients had thrown. He'd had too many cocktails. His head throbbed from all the booze. Damn it! What had happened?

He closed his eyes and took a deep breath.

Think, Peter. Where the heck are you? What happened?

But his head was empty. He tried frantically to summon some image that might help him. But all he could come up with was: Heat. Darkness. Emptiness.

.   .   .

Matthias Kronberg furiously swept the bank statements off his desk. His financial ruin was imminent. How would he explain this to his wife? He had roughly three weeks to cover his debts. If he didn't come up with a solution by then, he'd have to declare bankruptcy. How had he let this happen?

His father had built the company into a good-sized family business, and Matthias had taken the lead after his father had had a stroke eight years ago. They produced appliances for the world's largest aluminum-roll mill and had been among the German market leaders in the industry for decades. Business was as good as ever. Granted, there had been a steady decrease in sales in some areas in the past few years because of the Opel crisis and the low sales figures of the German automobile industry. But up until now, Matthias had managed to balance out the decrease in revenue with an increase in productivity. He'd also bought certain products from China and India, thereby saving the company a good deal of money.

His mother would turn over in her grave if she knew he had put the family's wealth at risk. Though ashamed to feel this way, he was thankful she was not around to learn of his many missteps. He could almost hear her hysterical voice, yelling at him that his brother would never have been so careless. His saintly brother, who didn't have the slightest clue what it meant to run a family business all alone. Sebastian had committed himself to the church from an early age and gone on to live as a monk in the monastery of Knechtsteden Abbey. Matthias, too, had had other interests in his youth, but since he was the firstborn, he'd had no choice but to step up and take over the business.

He glanced at his watch. Almost three o'clock in the afternoon. His new financial adviser would arrive any minute. Matthias quickly went to the bathroom and straightened his tie. When he saw his reflection in the mirror, he froze at the sight of the stranger staring back at him. He had gained several pounds because of the stress of the past few months. His face looked bloated, his cheeks flushed, and heavy bags sagged under his deep-set, grayish-blue eyes. Apart from his cheeks, his skin looked unnaturally dull. Countless gray streaks blemished his once-glorious head of brown hair. His age, his unhealthy lifestyle, and the stress had clearly left their marks.

Regardless, he would have to make a good impression with the new financial adviser. After all, she was his last hope.

·　·　·

The GPS had failed Anna once again and directed her to the wrong exit on the Autobahn. She didn't like taking the fifteen-mile detour through unfamiliar streets, but there was nothing she could do. It was almost three o'clock; she was running late for her appointment with her new client.

She knew very well that Herr Kronberg did not have the required credit score—the data from the Risk Management Department had made that perfectly clear. But she desperately needed a new client. If she did not reach her target, she could forget about her long-coveted bonus. Maybe she could close a cross-selling deal. After all, her boss was all gung ho about that sort of fashionable business.

Thirty minutes later, Anna reached her destination and parked. Weeds were growing everywhere in the cracks. It was obvious nobody had done maintenance here for a while, but the office building seemed to be in good shape, albeit in a distinct seventies architectural style. Sparkling-clean windows reflected the bright sunlight.

Anna put a hand to her forehead to shade her eyes from the sun, grabbed her manila folders from the passenger's seat, and skimmed the client's profile again. This meeting would not be easy. She had inherited Herr Kronberg from a coworker who had been fired a few weeks earlier. The majority of his clients had gone bankrupt because he had sold them overly risky structured products, especially so-called currency-related swaps that did not correspond at all to the needs of the respective clients.

Anna glanced over her new client's liquidity analysis. Hope was dim. Still, maybe she could help him. She got out of her car and walked confidently to the main entrance.

Behind the mirrored automatic door, a receptionist in her early fifties greeted Anna with a lackluster smile. She didn't come across as a great company representative. Her hair was drab, and her skin was ashen. The receptionist looked at Anna with utter indifference and said in a robotic voice, "Herr Kronberg is expecting you."

.   .   .

One hour later, Matthias Kronberg stood at the window of his office and watched Anna as she got into her car. Anna Winterfeld was the hottest financial adviser the bank had ever sent his way. She had tried her best to help him. She had proposed various plans that were all supposed to make up for her coworker's previous mistakes. He had almost liked her. But deep inside him emerged a strident voice with a thunderous warning: *Don't let her looks fool you. Bankers are all the same. No matter how nice they seem, all they're after is your money, and when you're down and out they won't be there for you!*

Still, his feelings contradicted the warning voice. "But Anna Winterfeld's different, really," he muttered to himself. "How could those big green eyes lie? No. Never!"

Don't be fooled by her, you idiot! She's like all the others. She doesn't deserve to walk this Earth. She violates the Lord's commandments!

"Nonsense. I like her, and somehow, I trust her."

He turned away from the window. Chaotic thoughts were racing through his throbbing head. Tired, he rubbed his temples. He paused for a moment, crossed himself, and made a call.

"Please tell Brother Sebastianus to call me at his earliest convenience."

He stood there for a few seconds with the receiver pressed to his ear, listening to the echoing chorales of the monks, the music spreading out in the background like a soothing wave. He wondered whether his brother's voice was among the pious singers, before he finally put down the receiver. There had been a faint click on the line, but Matthias hadn't noticed it.

.   .   .

Sebastian Kronberg, known as Brother Sebastianus to his fellow monks at the monastery in Knechtsteden, let out a deep sigh and pushed the "Escape" key on his laptop. He had heard enough. Matthias was going to need money in order to fend off the definite closure of the company. The financial adviser's proposals weren't bad, but without putting in some capital, there was no chance.

Sebastian thought back over the past few years. How many times had he pitched in to help his brother? He always worked behind the scenes, so that Matthias ended up believing he had managed the crisis himself. It was Sebastian who had legal authority over the family assets that had been invested in a foundation after their father's retirement eight years ago. Monks were not usually allowed to own assets, but a generous donation to the monastery and a few other tricks had facilitated the exception. Years before she had passed away, his mother had made it clear to Sebastian that he was to look after his brother, and she had made him reiterate that promise on her deathbed. Sebastian had kept his promise for years.

He tenderly stroked his laptop. He simply loved computers. Long before he had devoted himself to the Lord, programming had been his passion. He could hack into any system, and his talent allowed him to lead the life of a monk and simultaneously watch over his brother. Matthias had not the slightest idea that Sebastian was monitoring every aspect of his life—and had been for years. In fact, there were bugs and cameras everywhere. Modern technology certainly could work miracles!

V
Five Hundred Years Ago

Bastian hurried through the dark, narrow alleys of Zons. Despite the late hour, the air was still warm, and a soft, pleasant breeze drifted through the city. Under the clear night sky, the oppressive heat of the day had subsided. It wasn't far to the little house adjacent to the *Mühlenturm*, the Miller's Tower of Zons, where Bastian lived with Marie.

As he turned onto Zehntgasse, Bastian noticed the dark silhouette of someone scurrying at the end of the alley. Soon after, a light flickered. Now Bastian recognized Bechtolt, the night watchman, on his usual route with his lantern, making sure Zons was quiet, calm, and safe. The watchman blew his horn and began to sing his familiar song: *"Listen, folks, I tell you truly, our church clock has struck ten times! Ten commandments from God that we must obey! God watches over us, God protects us. Lord, in Your mercy and power, let this night be safe."*

The night watchman was shrouded in a long, dark coat and wore a black felt hat. Unlike the felt hats of the Fraternity of Saint Sebastian, his was not pointy. He held a lantern in his right hand and a lance in his left.

"Greetings, Bechtolt!"

A black patch covered Bechtolt's left eye. He gave Bastian a friendly look. Bechtolt used to be a sailor, and the many years of staring into the glistening sunlight while navigating the endless oceans had left him half-blind. When he grew too old to sail, he came to Zons, where his salary as a night watchman allowed him to carve out a modest existence. He was a real ruffian, well suited for the job. The drunks and troublemakers he picked up off the streets hardly ever resisted. Even though he was old now, Bechtolt was still huge and intimidating.

"Greetings to you, Bastian!"

The night watchman looked over Bastian's tall, muscular figure. He vividly remembered the curious young boy who'd diligently studied how to read and write with Father Johannes. Back then, he was petite, and his father entertained the idea of sending bright little Bastian to the cloister and making a scholar out of him. He seemed ill suited to be a miller. But soon Bastian grew tall and broad, towering above all the other kids his age. More recently, the valor and courage he had shown during the fatal-puzzle murder case had turned him into a local celebrity, stirring the hearts of many young women. When word spread of his marriage to Marie, more than a few of them harbored jealous thoughts; some even wished for Marie to die in childbirth, thereby bringing the attractive widower from the Zons City Guard back on the market. But Bechtolt knew the young man to be steady and loyal. He would always love Marie.

"The Council of the Seven Arrows is having a meeting at the tavern," Bastian said. "Did you see them coming?"

"No, but I did see one of them scurrying down the alley just now, right behind you. I thought you'd left the tavern with him."

"No," Bastian said, surprised. "When I left, they were all huddled together at a table. There was a lot of whispering going on."

"Oh, well, maybe I'm wrong. You have a good night, now."

27

The night watchman resumed his patrol, and Bastian continued toward Schlossstraße. An occasional cloud would drift through the sky and hide the starlight. Here or there Bastian thought he saw someone's silhouette, but he figured the night was only playing tricks on him. When he was just about to turn onto Schlossstraße, he heard a gurgling sound coming from a nook inside the outer wall of a nearby house. He wondered if his senses were fooling him again. Nevertheless, he paused and listened carefully.

There it was again. Now he was positive he had heard something. Bastian slowly approached the corner away from the streetlights, where it was pitch-dark. He couldn't see his hands in front of his face.

Silence.

He kept listening.

Silence.

Then, that gurgling sound. Bastian nearly tripped over something and stopped. His heart racing, he bent down to feel for what had tripped him and touched a rough cloth.

Again, the gurgling sound. Bastian jumped.

Oh my God, he thought. *Someone's lying here.*

With some effort, Bastian pulled the body out of the dark nook into the middle of the alley, where there was more light. He saw a black cloak and a pointed, black felt hat. The man painstakingly lifted his head and tried to speak, but his throat produced nothing but the now-familiar gurgling sound. Bastian bent down and tried to understand what the wounded man, whose strength was clearly waning, was trying to tell him.

"Keep the map safe!"

After that, the man's head sagged to the ground, and he took his last breath. When Bastian touched the dead man's throat, he felt a warm liquid.

Blood.

He could feel the outline of a long, gruesome cut. Someone must have sliced his throat!

The beam of a lantern illuminated the dead face, and Bastian recognized the man. It was Benedict, the standard-bearer of the Fraternity of Saint Sebastian. Bastian turned around and blinked into the bright light that had suddenly appeared behind him.

"What are you doing here in the darkness, Bastian?"

It was Jacob, the poor peon whose house looked like a patch-work quilt. He had come out of his ramshackle home and was peering over Bastian's shoulder.

His overall misery usually kept Jacob awake late into the night. Tossing and turning in bed as always, he had heard sounds outside. Finally, a strange shuffling had ended the slightest hope for sleep, and Jacob had made his way down the narrow stairs of his house and outside. He froze when he recognized Bastian bending over a dead body. Shocked and worried, he asked, "What happened?"

"I don't know, Jacob. Please, help me get him off the street."

. . .

That night Bastian, too, slept badly. In his dreams, he ran along Zehntgasse over and over again, trying to identify the shadow figure he had seen just before the night watchman had appeared. He had left the tavern alone. Nobody had followed him. How could Benedict Eschenbach, the standard-bearer, have passed him without Bastian noticing? Why did someone cut his throat, and what were the man's last words supposed to mean? *Keep the map safe!* What kind of map could Benedict have been referring to?

Bastian rubbed his tired eyes and glanced to the side. Marie was sound asleep. He admired her pretty face and the blonde hair that shone like gold in the early-morning light. He slipped out of bed, careful not to wake her.

29

Half an hour later, Bastian and Josef Hesemann were standing in the small courtyard of the doctor's house on Grünwaldstraße. Benedict Eschenbach's body had been placed on a wooden table for inspection. They carefully examined the cut in his throat. It was so long it seemed to reach from one ear to the other. Only the spine and a few muscles were still holding the head and body together. By now, the blood had dried. Josef scratched at the blood-encrusted wound, and a dark, almost-black clot of hardened blood fell to the ground.

"Bastian, I must say, you scared me quite a bit when you told me about the body. For a second I thought it was my cousin Conrad. I still haven't heard from him. He probably just forgot our appointment and is now deeply immersed in prayer in the monastery."

Another chunk of encrusted blood dropped to the ground. Josef leaned forward to take a closer look.

"We'll have to clean the edges of the wound if we want to determine the murder weapon."

Bastian nodded and, without a word, went into the house. When he came back, he was carrying a bucket of water and some linen cloths. The two men began cleaning the edges of the wound. Josef studied the cut. He had seen many wounds, but this one was completely different; in all his years as a doctor in Zons, he had never seen anything like it. Neither a knife, a sword, nor even a lance could have caused this. Josef knew the patterns those instruments made. A sword, for example, caused wounds that were as deep yet thicker than this one, which was at best one-fifth of an inch thick. Additionally, it ran completely horizontal. Only a very skilled sword fighter would have the ability to make such an exact cut. Besides, assuming the victim had defended himself, the sword became a very unlikely murder weapon.

Josef couldn't think of any weapon that matched this kind of cut. Its point of entry lay deeper on the left than where it exited, on the right. The doctor grabbed the bloodstained cloth they had used to clean the wound and turned the head of the body as far to the left as possible. The sight horrified Bastian. His stomach revolted, and he tried to focus only on the doctor. Josef seemed unaffected by the gruesome sight. His experienced hands examined the smooth edges of the wound. The weapon had cut through the larynx, which was now dangling lopsided in the lower part of the throat. The sinews, muscles, and blood vessels were equally cut through in such a smooth manner that it was easy to imagine they would simply grow together again if one were to reattach the head to the neck.

Josef bent as low as he could in order to examine Benedict's cervical spine from the front. The blade had scratched the bone. Here, too, the scratch lay deeper on the left side of the spine. They were clearly dealing with a smooth blade, not a serrated one. And suddenly, Josef had the answer: a sickle! When he was a young boy, his uncle had taught him how to cut grass and grains with this tool. One hand held a bundle of grass or grain, the other held the sickle. One would then cut through the stalks beneath the hand in a single, smooth, circular movement. It was important to apply the sickle correctly if one wanted to cut through all the stalks neatly—just as Benedict Eschenbach's throat had been cut.

The doctor had learned two things: what kind of weapon they were looking for and that the murderer must be left-handed. That explained why the blade's point of entry lay deeper than the point of exit. He relayed his findings to Bastian while touching the throat's muscle tissue with his fingers. When he came across something hard, he stopped. With his other hand, he gently separated the muscles and sinews.

"Look and see, Bastian. I found something that doesn't belong here."

Curious, Bastian came closer. By now his stomach had calmed down and he could endure the gruesome sight a little better. He saw a necklace stuck inside the pharynx.

"Get hold of that for me, will you, please? I don't want it to fall down even deeper, because then we'll have to open up the entire pharynx," said the doctor. Disgusted, Bastian reached inside the dead man's throat, hoping he could get a hold of the necklace with his fingertips. But it was very slick, and he had to reach farther in. Josef opened the wound as wide as possible. Bastian slowly pulled the necklace out and held it up. A key dangled from the chain.

"Did we not see something like this last night in the Old Hen Tavern?"

"Quite possibly! But how did it end up in Benedict's throat?"

"He must have swallowed it."

"Probably just before he was murdered. Otherwise it would have gone to his stomach, or he might have thrown it up," Josef said. "It didn't get farther down because he died."

Bastian watched the key dangle in front of his eyes. In his mind he saw Benedict lying on the street, rattling and wheezing. He had wanted to tell Bastian something.

"Keep the map safe!"

"What did you say?"

"'Keep the map safe.' Those were his last words. I could barely hear them."

"Maybe he swallowed the key to hide it from the killer!" Josef's voice grew louder.

"That's it! The tavern was packed yesterday. Many people would have seen the key. The murderer might have been among the patrons."

"Right! And Wernhart talked about the three keys and the chest for half the night. I bet he's not the only one who knows about it."

"Or what's in it . . ."

"The treasure of the Fraternity of Saint Sebastian!"

VI
Present

He eyed the golden sickle in awe. It rested on a soft velvet cloth folded within an ancient, jewel-adorned chest. He let his fingers run over the blade, which was still razor sharp. He felt sublime. He had been chosen to guard this precious work of art, which had remained intact and undiscovered throughout the centuries. They had chosen him because he had proven himself to be worthy. Only the best of the truly worthy could become a *guardian*.

He took the sickle in his hand. The golden blade reflected the light from the dim lamp, and a bright glimmer filled the small, dusty room where he kept his treasures. He sliced through the air, and the sickle hissed with each majestic movement. It felt like the object belonged in his hand.

He paused. His heart was racing as he practiced swift, precise martial-arts techniques. He had long prepared for what now seemed within reach. But the time was not quite right yet. He had to be patient and wait for the right moment. He let out a small sigh of disappointment and put the sickle back onto its velvet cloth inside the chest. He made sure that the chest was thoroughly locked before putting it back into the secret safe, hidden behind a huge painting.

"Gentlemen, you don't seem to be grasping the gravity of the situation!" Hans Steuermark fought hard to keep his anger at bay. His two best detectives sat in front of him, staring at the floor.

"The media is outside waiting for me, and I demand you give me something to feed them! It can't be this difficult to find the body!"

"Yeah, right," Oliver muttered under his breath. It *shouldn't* be that difficult, especially when the body had most likely been in contact with hydrochloric acid. Over the past two weeks, they had been utterly meticulous in their work. They had checked the order books of every German supplier of hydrochloric acid, but they hadn't found anything suspicious. Scrutiny of all missing-person reports had proven equally fruitless. All they knew from the lab report was that the bones probably belonged to an adult between forty and fifty years old. The layers of cartilage showed the first symptoms of aging. And because the bones were fairly large, it seemed highly improbable that the victim was female. They were looking for a middle-aged man.

Initially, they concentrated on five missing persons who in one way or another matched the lab results. They thoroughly vetted each person's social and professional contacts, but that hadn't produced a lead. They might have found one clue. But as incensed as Steuermark was, there wasn't much of a chance to speak with him rationally.

Steuermark paced the room. Oliver watched his boss, a tall, haggard man with sharp eyes that sparkled like multifaceted jewels when he was livid. Steuermark abruptly stopped.

"I really would like to know what's inside your little head, Bergmann!"

Oliver swallowed hard and his Adam's apple bobbed up and down. He winced when his cell phone beeped twice. A text message. He pulled the phone from his pocket and read the message.

It's my day off! Lunch at Magnus, 1pm?

Oliver beamed. A text from Emily. When he looked up again, he met the angry stare of Hans Steuermark.

"Bergmann, I didn't promote you because you're so good at forgetting your duties when you're infatuated. While I agree with you that Emily Richter is indeed very lovely and provided us with indispensable and decisive information during the fatal-puzzle murder case, I do urge you to go about your private life outside of business hours!"

Embarrassed, Oliver bowed his head and put the phone back in his pocket. Klaus chuckled. Steuermark turned his head with a jerk. Now he focused on Klaus, who stopped chuckling.

Oliver cleared his throat and tried to rescue the situation by relaying what they had found out about the missing persons. "So far we've narrowed our investigation down to five potential victims." Oliver opened the binder that rested on his lap and, one after the other, put photocopies of five profiles on Steuermark's desk. "The first person here was reported missing six months ago. Peter Schreiner, who disappeared after a vacation he'd taken with his wife. He's forty-six and works as a mechanic at a garage in Dormagen."

Oliver ran a finger over the paper. The photo showed a suntanned, portly man wearing rimless glasses. A significant amount of money from the couple's joint account had gone missing along with him, so it seemed rather unlikely that Peter Schreiner was the victim of a crime. Oliver imagined him basking on an exotic beach in the company of a lover half his age while the police still had to do their grunt work.

The second profile was more promising. Markus Heilkamp, a forty-nine-year-old chemist who worked for a large chemical plant in Dormagen, had disappeared three months ago. Divorced, he lived by himself on a small farm on the outskirts of Zons. He had disappeared without any kind of notice. He had come to work the same as every other day, left around six in the evening, and disappeared without a trace. What was particularly interesting about Markus Heilkamp was that he had been in charge of the new world-class plant, which the huge parent company had recently built at the beginning of the year for €150 million. It was going to produce so-called TDI products—from toluene diisocyanate—which were essential for the manufacture of polyurethane foam, often used for cold-foam mattresses and car seats. The group had generated quite a PR circus around the financing of the new plant. One thing Oliver remembered vividly was that hydrochloric acid was one of the by-products of this chemical process.

The foot bones they had found had been in contact with hydrochloric acid. The thought alone made Oliver's own feet and hands tingle. Did the foot belong to Markus Heilkamp, the chemist? How easy was it to make a person disappear in one of the huge hydrochloric-acid tanks inside the plant? Oliver made a note to himself. He would like to dig deeper there.

While Oliver filled Hans Steuermark in on the background facts, he was relieved to see that the chief inspector was relaxing—probably, Oliver assumed, because Steuermark already imagined the impending press conference and how he would impress the journalists, now that he could finally present a somewhat-promising lead. Even without substantial evidence, they might be on to something and could maybe even find the body. Oliver didn't believe in coincidences when it came to a murder case.

Oliver threw a quick glance at Klaus. Klaus was a veteran with the crime division; he stared out the window, utterly bored. His expression conveyed indifference. There was nothing that Klaus cared less about than tasks related to lab analysis. So they had found a bone. Now what? It could mean all sorts of things. Or nothing. His element was the street, investigating the crime scene. He preferred talking to people instead of researching for hours online, or, even worse, rummaging through books and newspaper archives. Klaus was convinced that every perpetrator would eventually give himself away; it was simply a matter of skilled questioning techniques. Klaus also liked being the center of attention during interrogations. That was why Oliver and Klaus made such a perfect team. Oliver wasn't necessarily enthusiastic about research work, either. But he vetted each and every available source, even if that meant hours and hours in front of the computer—as long as it allowed him to find that one piece of information that would untangle the mystery of a new case. Unlike Klaus, Oliver actually enjoyed working systematically behind the scenes, through a chain of circumstantial evidence, instead of having to listen to an endless parade of witnesses.

Oliver looked at the profile of the third missing person, a forty-nine-year-old man named Peter Hirschauer. He had disappeared a little over two months ago. A successful banker who had counseled many renowned clients, his disappearance seemed incomprehensible at first glance. But when Oliver found out that Hirschauer had been fired prior to his disappearance, things seemed to make a little more sense. But the bank refused to cooperate unless a proper investigation took place.

Dimitri Orlow and Vladimir Tereschenko were numbers four and five on the list. Both had verified links to the Russian Mafia. The crime organization's brutality and tendency to make victims disappear were well known, which was why Oliver closely considered both men as leads. He wouldn't be surprised if the bone fragments were all that remained of them. Fortunately, he had found DNA samples from both men in the criminal-records database. The lab was still running some tests, and Oliver expected to know in a few days whether the bones matched Orlow's or Tereschenko's DNA.

Frowning, Hans Steuermark reached for the profile of Markus Heilkamp, the man who had worked for the chemical plant.

"I want you to find out everything about him. Turn over every stone from his work life and private life. This is the top priority!"

.   .   .

He stared at the menu of the McDonald's drive-through, near a chain supermarket in Dormagen. The many colorful images confused him, and, despite his thick glasses, the tiny font made it difficult for him to read the menu. He didn't know what to order. On his previous visit, it had taken him so long to decide that the drivers behind him had honked. Then he had settled for chicken nuggets, because they were at the top of the menu and the only thing he could decipher. But he hadn't liked the small fried-meat bites that were supposed to taste like chicken breast.

He wasn't here for the food, anyway. Her shift began at eleven every Tuesday morning, and he had arrived at eleven on the dot. At this hour, between breakfast and lunch, nobody wanted to order anything, and the drive-through was usually empty. He took off his heavy, horn-rimmed glasses and reached for his handkerchief. He had never frequented fast-food restaurants before he'd found her. Why couldn't she work in a diner? There, he could sit comfortably at a table, taking in her lovely face while she delighted him with her beautiful smile. He pictured her, serving plate in hand, bending down at his table to arrange the dishes. He would lean forward ever so slightly, hoping to brush her arm, to feel her sweet breath on his face . . .

"Can I take your order, please?"

The loudspeaker next to the menu crackled and brought him back to reality. He enjoyed the tone of her friendly voice, despite the static. He wiped the sweat from his forehead, put his glasses back on, and checked his appearance in the rearview mirror. A greasy, gray streak of hair had fallen onto his forehead. He hastily stroked it back.

"Miss, I'd like that Mc . . . um . . ." He faltered and tried to concentrate on the writing. What did the menu say?

"Pardon, I didn't hear you. Could you repeat your order, please?"

"Sure." He blinked. "Um, the McRib meal, I'd like to order the McRib meal."

"Regular, large, or supersized?"

What did they want from him with all these different sizes—a regular meal wouldn't do?

"Supersized, please."

"Mayonnaise or ketchup with the french fries?"

I'd rather no french fries at all, he thought, but then said: "Ketchup, please."

"What did you want to drink?"

"What do you recommend, miss?"

"Coke, Diet Coke, Dr Pepper, Sprite, or mineral water."

Her words rattled through his brain like machine-gun fire. He understood nothing. He was lost. Now he simply had to avoid embarrassing himself. He was almost done. *Focus, Dietrich! What exactly did she just say?* Luckily, he remembered. Mineral water. That was it.

"Mineral water, please."

"That'll be five euros and seventy-nine cents. Please drive up to the second window."

Good Lord, he had made it. Soon he would see her pretty face! He paused to take a deep breath. He mustn't panic now. He wanted to savor this moment as fully as possible. Slowly he pushed his foot down on the gas, and his old Ford glided up to the second window.

"Five seventy-nine, please."

A young woman with rosy cheeks, blonde braids, and sparkling blue eyes smiled at him. His mind went blank. Her resemblance to Marie, Bastian Mühlenberg's wife, was startling and took his breath away each time he saw her. He glanced briefly at the small plastic name tag pinned above her chest. In black letters it read "Sandra Schwanengel," but he chose to ignore that. For him, her name was Marie.

Dietrich handed her a ten. He could have given her the exact amount, but this way, he got to touch her twice. He eyed her seductively when she handed him the change. And just the touch of her fingers made his desire for her youthful, shapely body spring to life in his pants.

"Please drive up to the next window!"

With those words, she slid the glass closed and disappeared. Dietrich sighed and drove up to the next window, faster than before. There wasn't anything worth looking at now. A young man handed him a brown paper bag with his supersized McRib meal and a damp paper cup of water. Dietrich rolled up the squeaky window of his shabby old car and drove back to Zons, to his second home at Schlossstraße 1, where the Neuss County Archive was located. For thirty years, Dietrich Hellenbruch had been working as the county's archivist inside the old walls of the former Burg Friedestrom.

.   .   .

A pile of books that had been sitting on the windowsill tumbled to the floor.

"Careful!" Emily moaned in Oliver's ear.

They had quickly gulped down their lunch at Magnus, a popular student hangout in Cologne, and had stumbled up the stairs to Emily's apartment. They hadn't even stopped kissing while Emily searched her purse for her keys, and they had rushed into the bedroom as soon as the door was opened.

With his strong body, Oliver pressed Emily against the wall and firmly grabbed her butt with his hands. He pushed her farther up and pressed himself between her thighs, spreading her legs open. His pants were painfully tight in the crotch. Oliver longed to tear her clothes off, but a small voice in the back of his head reminded him how fragile and petite she was. He couldn't act rough. He had to be tender. He panted, leaned back a little, and looked at her face. Her cheeks were flushed, and her eyes were closed until she opened them and smiled.

"You need to get back to the office?"

"Yes. But you know I'd rather stay with you."

He glanced at his watch. Damn it, he had to be back at Headquarters in half an hour. Hans Steuermark would go berserk if he was late. But then, he just couldn't let go of this sweet, sexy embrace. He inhaled Emily's lovely perfume, which he would recognize anywhere. Her thighs pressed against his, and he didn't want this moment to end. He powerfully thrust Emily back against the wall. He could hardly control himself. Only a sudden vibration made him pause. His cell phone was ringing. Oliver groaned and reached for the phone in his pocket. *Oh no—of all people and moments, not her, not now.* His mother was calling. What did she want now?

"Sorry, Emily, but I have to take this." He let out a deep sigh and answered. "Hi, Mom, what's up?"

Since his father's death a year ago, his mother had lived alone in the big house where Oliver had grown up. He wished it weren't an hour away from Neuss. Being closer would make it easier for him to look in on his mother more regularly and perhaps cut down on her constant calls.

"Oliver, the basement window is broken. There's a hole as big as a brick, and there are shards and splinters everywhere. Should I call the police?"

"No, Mom, that's not necessary. I'll take care of it. Don't worry. Remember, your son's with the police."

His last sentence made him grin. His mother was terribly proud of him for being a detective, but since his position didn't require him to wear a uniform, his mother didn't see him as a real cop. It was difficult for her to relinquish the image of the German street cop clad in his blue uniform.

Oliver quickly ended the call. He would send over an officer from the patrol division. He was sure the windowpane had merely succumbed to age, but he knew his mother would feel better once a "real" cop had inspected the scene. He looked again at his watch. He really had to run. He gave Emily a deep kiss and said good-bye.

"I'll call you later!"

He grabbed his stuff and hurried down the stairs. As soon as he got in his car, his phone rang again. This time it was Klaus.

"Hey, buddy, where are you? Did you forget the meeting?"

"No, been busy."

"Ah, *busy*, that's what they call it nowadays. How exactly 'busy' were you with Emily?" Oliver could clearly hear Klaus's grin.

"Listen, just come up with something in case Steuermark gets there before me."

"Of course, what'd you expect? I already got you covered with the perfect alibi. We have an appointment at the chemical plant in Dormagen. So hurry over and pick me up."

Klaus hung up before Oliver had a chance to thank him. Oliver raced along the Autobahn toward Neuss.

.   .   .

Emily picked up the books that had fallen to the floor. Most of them she had used last year, while researching her feature series about the historic Zons murder cases in 1495. Her best friend, Anna, had barely escaped the copycat killer who had replayed the fatal puzzle from the past.

Emily was looking forward to her meeting with Anna tonight. They had a lot to catch up on. The editor at the local newspaper, the *Rheinische Post*, had offered Emily a follow-up assignment. He wanted her to write about another grim serial killer who had terrorized medieval Zons. She had hoped for just this kind of offer. Her first assignment, covering the fatal-puzzle murders from over five hundred years ago, had been a big success. Pride and excitement pulsed through her. New ideas were already forming, and she needed Anna's opinion.

Emily paused when thoughts of Oliver overwhelmed her. She was still shivering from his passionate kisses. Lost in her thoughts, she didn't notice the small, old piece of parchment that slipped from the books in her hands and wafted down to the floor, coming to rest under the radiator beneath the window. She put the books back on the windowsill, took out her phone, and called Anna.

.   .   .

Peter had determined that he was trapped inside the trunk of a car. That explained the unbearable heat, the stuffy air, and the small crack of light that, at least during the day, reassured him he was still alive. He had long lost count of the days he had been held captive. Between excruciatingly long intervals, someone opened the trunk and brutal hands tore the gag from his mouth, shoved a tube as thin as a straw deep inside his throat, and fed him liquid that kept him alive. Peter suspected it was a high-protein drink; after each feeding, he didn't feel hungry or thirsty for hours. His kidnapper had also made sure his other needs were met. A bladder bag attached to a catheter, and a small plastic bag taped to his anus, prevented him from having to lie in his own filth and excrement.

How thoughtful, Peter thought sarcastically while trying to roll into a slightly different position, which caused him a lot of pain. His skin was swollen from the heat and sore from the rough material that covered the bottom of the trunk. It was useless; he could barely move. He heard a muffled squeaking noise outside and listened intently. The squeaking sound came closer and stopped. A force pressed down on the car from above, and then there was a jolt. At first he hadn't been able to determine what was causing the squeaking noises, but then he knew what he was in for. The car began swinging left and right and was spun in all directions, lifted into the air, set down, and lifted again.

From farther away he heard again that muffled squeaking noise, metal on metal. Iron, rust, and steel being pressed together. The noise—probably from a scrap press—grew louder and louder. It sounded like an angry monster. Cars were being scrapped, and every time the crane lifted his car, it was moved gradually closer to the press. So this was how he would die? Crushed like a tiny fly between the claws of a steel monster?

Furious, he pulled together the last of his energy and drove his knees against the lid of the trunk as forcefully as he could.

Once. Twice. Nothing happened.

His knees throbbed from striking the unyielding metal. That was all he had achieved.

He tried again.

Click.

Peter didn't trust his ears. Had the trunk actually opened? Again he kneed the lid. It had opened! Glaring sunlight pierced his eyes.

The pain startled him, and he froze. His eyes weren't used to the sunlight, and his lungs took in the fresh air. An alien, indefinable sound escaped his throat. Blinded, he tried to feel along the edge of the trunk with his hands, but they were bound by handcuffs. His mobility was severely constricted, and he was too exhausted. He fell back into the trunk and took a moment to gather his strength. He knew he needed to escape as fast as he could.

VII
Five Hundred Years Ago

He leaned back against the cold, damp wall of the vault and didn't move. He had honed the art of moving about silently, becoming one with the background, for so long now that he began to think of himself as nearly invisible. His eyes had adapted to the darkness, and he could quietly observe the moaning man sitting on the chair of nails in the middle of the room.

Yesterday he had whipped him with his rod. At first he'd hit the naked body rather softly, but when his victim had begun whimpering, he'd grown angrier and whipped him harder. These liars had no respect. They neither took responsibility for their lies nor could endure the slightest pain. Had this liar accepted his punishment like an honorable man, he might have continued with the softer treatment. Maybe the leather straps would have sufficed. Maybe, seeing the man's tortured body, he would have felt that this liar had sufficiently repented for all his sins. Maybe he would have let him go. He didn't need to see him dead. God was all about giving life, not taking it. But penance had to be done!

The thought aroused him. He felt hot, vicious wrath rise inside him. In this moment there was only one thing he wanted: to beat all the lies out of this godless sinner. But he had to be patient. He needed to calm down. It was not the time yet.

The man's moaning was fusing with the chants he had learned as a little boy. Often his beloved choir had gathered around the big altar and intoned this dear melody. It was a balm for his agitated mind. His arousal ebbed. He regained his composure and listened intently to the familiar, comforting melody accompanied by the moaning man on the chair of nails.

.   .   .

"Promise me, Bastian, please." His brother's voice was frail and hoarse. Heinrich coughed and, exhausted, sank back against the large pillows that were propped up behind him. Today he was feeling particularly bad. It must have been partly a reaction to the stuffy humidity that had been paralyzing Zons for weeks. For some inhabitants, breathing was a strain and the slightest movement was arduous.

Bastian looked at his older brother with concern. Heinrich had always been his hero, a muscular guy so tall he seemed larger than life. He made lifting heavy bags of flour look like lifting feather pillows. But the years of breathing in fine dust particles from the flour and grindstones had damaged his lungs. They couldn't take in the amount of oxygen needed to keep Heinrich's muscular body going. An early death was common among millers, due to the hard and unhealthy work conditions.

Bastian quickly set aside this disturbing thought. *No.* This was his strong brother Heinrich, who always bounced back.

"Heinrich, I shall gladly make that promise, once the time comes. But it hasn't come yet!"

"Father Johannes visited with me this morning. He advised me to ask you, Bastian. I'm very sorry, but I'm afraid I don't have much time left, and I want you to fulfill my last wish."

Bastian didn't want to hear this. But he couldn't ignore the seriousness in his brother's eyes. He sighed. "Well then, Heinrich, I promise. I shall have you buried in the cemetery of Knechtsteden Abbey, where our brother Albrecht lives."

Heinrich smiled. "Thank you, Brother. I know you will keep your promise."

"Yes. But don't think your wish is about to come true just yet. You are tough; I know you will recover. I bet next week you'll be back at the mill, carrying bags of flour." Bastian tried to be cheerful, but even he couldn't help but notice his brother's gray face and dull, hollow eyes. He was overcome by a sudden, gigantic fear. He couldn't force a smile; he gently patted Heinrich's shoulder as he said good-bye.

.   .   .

Bastian gazed up into the sky. The sun was rising rapidly. If he wanted to speak with Father Johannes before mass, he'd have to hurry. Mass started in an hour. Bastian paced the narrow alleys. He wanted to have enough time to show Father Johannes the silver necklace he and the doctor had found inside Benedict Eschenbach's throat.

Despite the rush, his thoughts wandered back to Heinrich. It depressed him that his brother thought he was dying. Moreover, Heinrich had never been particularly interested in religion—so it seemed strange to Bastian that it was so important to him to be buried in the monastery's cemetery. He tried to put himself in Heinrich's place. Would he want to be buried in such a foreign environment? No! His place was alongside his wife, Marie. Bastian wondered why so many of Zons's citizens had suddenly turned to God and religion. It had all started when Master Huppertz Helpenstein took charge of the Fraternity of Saint Sebastian, and piety had become increasingly more important than martial arts and archery.

Then Bastian's thoughts turned to his middle brother, Albrecht, and he had a hard time remembering his face. Because their father didn't have the financial means to provide adequately for all six of his sons, it had been decided that little Albrecht was to become a monk. He'd entered Knechtsteden Abbey when he was only eight years old. Bastian had been only five then, but he vividly remembered how much Heinrich had suffered. Technically, the monastery wasn't far away from Zons, but the monks followed strict rules and hardly ever granted their novices contact with the secular world. Heinrich had always been very protective of the boy with the sickly nature, which left Bastian craving the same amount of attention and care that was poured over fragile Albrecht.

·   ·   ·

Knechtsteden Abbey, 1478, eighteen years earlier

Frightened, the little boy looked up at the men clad in their impressive cloaks. The long, woven-wool garments floated around their legs. They walked into the chapel and stopped in front of the decorative altar. They began chanting a melody that touched and caressed the little boy's heart in a most marvelous way. Never would this tune leave his memory. He would always be able to find it in his deepest, innermost feelings. He wasn't frightened anymore. From now on, he was one of those men, whose voices, years before him, had brought this wonderful melody to life and filled the cold halls and corridors of the abbey with this divine masterpiece.

Two other little boys stood next to him. They seemed to be having similar feelings. Their eyes shone, and a soft pink covered their pale young cheeks. Clearly, God had led them here!

.　　.　　.

Knechtsteden Abbey, 1490

Twelve years after he had entered the monastery, Albrecht knew that not everyone treated the chapel, in which he had first heard the marvelous melody, with the reverence appropriate to a holy place. Over the past few weeks he had learned what hate was—profound, soul-eating hate. Albrecht, Huppertz, and Conrad had developed one common enemy. Ever since they had stepped over Knechtsteden's threshold as scared little boys, they had been instructed to open their hearts to God and do good deeds. But when that blasphemous seller of indulgences, Johann Tetzel, had appeared, the three friends knew immediately that he was not walking in God's way. He shunned and desecrated every rule that Brother Ignatius had taught them.

Especially the three rules that had to be observed during confessions. Brother Ignatius had repeated them so often, Albrecht could have recited them standing on his head. First, *contritio cordis*, the true contrition of the heart. Second, *confessio oris*, the detailed and verbal confession of each and every sin. And finally, *satisfactio operis*, satisfaction through good deeds. A sinner had to truly feel remorse, then verbally list all his transgressions, and finally gain atonement by doing good.

Johann Tetzel, however, made a bargain with the mercy of the Lord. He sold indulgence letters and thus earned himself many thousands of guldens. When the three young monks first heard one of Tetzel's indulgence sermons, they were appalled. Johann Tetzel was a savvy and engaging speaker, but he haughtily paraded up and down on his little pedestal, his chest swollen with pride, his piercing blue eyes looking down on the people crowded around him. He had branded himself an unquestionable representative of God on Earth. When he preached the Lord's words with his deep, sonorous, confidence-inspiring voice, he made it seem like a gesture of charity, and everyone was entranced. To their astonishment, the three young monks heard that a sinner didn't need to confess his sins to a preacher but that he could atone for his sins by buying a letter of indulgence instead. When Tetzel had uttered those abhorrent words, Albrecht heard a deep sigh and turned around to see Brother Ignatius crossing himself, shaking his head in disbelief. How was that supposed to work, to atone for sins without confessing?

Undeterred in his confidence despite the monks' show of disapproval, Johann Tetzel proceeded to present to the awed crowd a large chest on which the Devil was painted wearing a heinous grimace while he tortured the poor souls of sinners in purgatory. Above the dramatic illustration, big golden letters read: "Keep Your Soul Out of the Fire by Putting Money in the Box."

The crowd erupted and immediately formed a long line. Everyone wanted to buy letters of indulgence for themselves or their deceased relatives. Soon the chest was filled to the brim with guldens and so heavy that two monks struggled to carry it off the pedestal. The crowd dispersed. Only the monks from Knechtsteden Abbey were left behind. They huddled in small groups, whispering excitedly. Johann Tetzel looked around and said, "Well, dear brothers, I hope you enjoyed my sermon!"

To the dismay of the monks, Abbot Ludwig von Monheim began clapping his hands as he hurried over to the preacher and patted his shoulder. Albrecht couldn't believe what he saw. He glanced at Huppertz and Conrad. Pale and inert, they watched the scene.

51

Brother Ignatius crossed himself again. His lips were trembling and his eyes grew furious.

The friends watched as young Johann Tetzel left the square in the company of the abbot, who cordially put his arm around Tetzel's shoulder as they walked toward the chapel. Apparently, Monheim was still very moved by the preacher's words. Albrecht thought Johann Tetzel must have been born with his greedy love for gold. The son of a prominent goldsmith, Tetzel hailed from the small village of Pirna, near Dresden. He had studied theology at the University of Leipzig, and only three years ago earned his Baccalaureus Artium degree. Exactly one year ago, he had entered the Dominican monastery of Saint Pauli in Leipzig, where they had welcomed him with open arms because of his obvious speaking talent. Soon enough, he took up his activity as an itinerant preacher promoting indulgences. The abbot at Knechtsteden Abbey had learned of Tetzel's impressive performances, and it had given him enormous satisfaction to book Tetzel for one of his famous sermons.

Ever since Burgundian troops had pillaged Knechtsteden Abbey in 1474, the monastery had been steeped in financial problems. The former abbot, Heinrich Schlickum, never got over the devastation of his dear abbey and died that same year. His successor, Ludwig von Monheim, was forced to rebuild Knechtsteden from the ashes. It was a very expensive endeavor, and by now, the once-filled coffers were always empty. The abbey desperately needed funds. So much so that, in the abbot's eyes, even the idea of offering indulgences for money no longer represented a sacrilege. Quite a few of the monks opposed the change at first, but empty coffers and survival instincts eventually forced them to adapt to the new situation. Little did they know that, only a few decades later, the selling of indulgences would compel the famous priest Martin Luther to write his *Ninety-Five Theses*, thus initiating a reform process that later resulted in

Pope Pius V deciding, in 1567, to cancel all grants of indulgences that involved any sort of financial transaction.

But nobody could anticipate the course of history. What counted currently was that the abbey desperately needed financial relief. The abbot was convinced that he acted for the benefit of everyone. After all, praying alone didn't feed hungry mouths. Still, the young and zealous monks didn't agree at all. They'd rather starve than violate divine commandments. Their young hearts beat for what they had been taught since childhood. They beat for God and mercy, certainly not for penance on sale in the bargain bins.

.   .   .

Bastian opened the heavy church door and stepped inside the cool, dark hall. What a refreshing respite from the humid air outside. Father Johannes had already changed for mass and was wearing his habit, adorned with precious stones. He stood at the altar and put new white candles into their holders.

"Greetings, Bastian. What brings you to my church at this early hour?"

"Father Johannes, I need to speak with you urgently."

Bastian pulled the silver necklace out of his pocket and showed it to the priest. An astonished sound escaped the clergyman's throat.

"Where did you get this?"

"Benedict Eschenbach, the standard-bearer of the fraternity, swallowed it."

"Swallowed it?"

"Benedict was killed last night. I was on my way home and found him shoved into a dark corner of Grünwaldstraße, right in front of old Jacob's house. Benedict was still alive. With the last of his strength he said, 'Keep the map safe.' Do you know what that means?"

Father Johannes motioned Bastian to follow him. With a pace that was surprisingly quick for his old age, he hurried into a small vestibule, its entrance hidden behind the altar. Once inside, he stopped abruptly. Bastian, following him closely, almost bumped into his friend and teacher. Father Johannes scratched his head and looked around as if searching for something.

"Where did I store it?" he muttered to himself. "Ah, yes, now I remember!"

He walked over to an old armoire in one corner and tried to push it to the side. Bastian came to his aid. At first, the heavy oak armoire didn't move an inch, but when Bastian flexed his muscles, the mighty piece of furniture scratched and squeaked across the ages-old stone floor. It probably hadn't been moved for centuries. Bastian saw huge cobwebs, and on the floor a large group of sow bugs scurried about to find the next dark place. Father Johannes didn't seem to notice the vermin. He reached through the spider-webs to the wall. There, he felt around until he found a small lever. He vigorously turned it up. Bastian heard a clicking sound, and the thick church wall swung open a crack. Father Johannes reached into the crack and pulled out an old linen shroud. It smelled dank and moldy.

Entranced, Bastian watched Father Johannes place the shroud on top of a small table and unfold it. A silver necklace appeared. Bastian couldn't believe his eyes: a key hung from the silver chain. The old priest gave Bastian a meaningful glance.

"I never expected this would happen in my lifetime. And that you, of all people, would bring me the key."

The priest's words didn't make any sense. What was the old man trying to tell him? Bastian stared at his mentor.

"Sit down, dear boy, and I shall share my secret with you. It's a secret that has been carried on from one generation to the next and will be revealed to you today, for you have come here with the silver key."

Bewildered, Bastian sat in a chair. What kind of secret did Johannes keep?

"More than a hundred years ago, Archbishop Friedrich von Saarwerden authorized Zons to levy a toll on ships transporting cargo on the river—a privilege formerly held by our considerably larger neighboring town of Neuss. He also decided to have Zons fortified and had a huge wall of basaltic rock erected around the town. The wall was supposed to protect the town and the customs revenues. Yet there was something else the archbishop wanted to protect. Friedrich von Saarwerden was aware that building the wall would take many years and that he wouldn't live to see the finished construction. So he assigned the priest with the safekeeping of his holiest of holies. From then on, the secret of the key on the silver necklace was transmitted from one priest to the next. Each clergyman in turn was commanded to keep the secret and defend it with his life, if need be. The secret must only be revealed when someone comes to the church and holds an identical key." The old priest let the silver key swing before his eyes. "Bastian, I'm sure you've heard that the treasure is kept in a chest that can only be opened when three keys are inserted in the chest's lock at the same time."

Bastian recalled Wernhart's words from the night before at the Old Hen Tavern. He vividly remembered seeing a key on a necklace handed across the table. It had to be the very same necklace he had pulled out of poor Benedict Eschenbach's throat the following morning.

"The fraternity and the priests are supposed to keep that chest safe. It must not be opened. That's why the three keys are stored in three different places. The day when two keys happen to be in the same place, the contents of the chest must be rescued, lest all three keys fall into the wrong hands—and with them, the archbishop's treasure. It's too high of a risk at this point."

"What secret is inside the chest? Can't the chest be opened by force?"

"If opened by force, the contents of the chest will automatically be destroyed. Inside the chest, on both sides, are delicate glass vials filled with acid. If the chest is forced open, the vials will spill out and immediately destroy the contents."

"All right, Father Johannes, I'm following. But what is so important that it must not be discovered?"

"My dear boy, I'll tell you when the time is right. For now, your next task is to bring me the third key. Once that's done, I shall tell you what to do." Father Johannes put the key back onto the linen shroud. Then he took the second key out of Bastian's hand and placed it next to the other. He wrapped the two keys in the shroud and carefully hid it inside the crack in the wall. He motioned Bastian to help him move the heavy armoire back to its original position. When this was done, Bastian stood inside the doorway, hoping he could coax Father Johannes into revealing more about the mysterious contents of the treasure chest. But the priest simply walked past him and admonished him: "Be patient, Bastian. I'll let you in on the secret soon enough. But first, bring me the third key!"

Father Johannes put the remaining candles into their holders. Bastian had followed him up to the altar. He didn't want to give in already. The priest couldn't possibly send him away like that. But Johannes busied himself with the last preparations for mass, paying no attention to his former disciple.

Eventually, Bastian left. He felt sullen. How was he supposed to find the third key when he didn't even know who might have it?

On his way out, he almost ran into Brother Ignatius. He was the priest's younger brother and had recently taken to visiting the church more regularly. Ignatius helped the older man with whatever needed to be done. Suddenly, Bastian's thoughts returned to his own brother, Albrecht. Maybe Ignatius could persuade Albrecht to come visit poor Heinrich. It could lift the sick man's spirits and hopefully quicken his recovery.

But first, he needed to consult with Wernhart. Maybe his friend could assist him in finding the third key.

VIII
Present

Cautiously, he inserted the third key into the lock. The lock was artfully hidden amid the wooden ornamentation and was very hard to see. Less-expert eyes than his might not even find it.

Click. The key fit perfectly. He turned it forty-five degrees, causing another clicking sound. Now it was unlocked. He would now be able to complete his magnum opus. His hands trembled with excitement as he took the golden sickle out of its chest. The loudspeakers behind him crackled. He turned his head to look at the monitor on the table next to him. He saw an old vehicle in a white-tiled room illuminated by glaring lights. The trap had snapped shut!

· · ·

Peter breathed. His heart pounded loud and fast, like jungle drums. If he wanted to get out of here, he needed to open his eyes and get his bearings. He hadn't kneed open that damn trunk lid for nothing! Carefully, he opened his eyes a little. Yes, better. The light was still glaring, but it didn't hurt as much as before. He waited a few seconds and looked around. The scenery beyond the edge of the trunk seemed rather benign. He saw white tiles with gray grout around them. He had been convinced he was in a scrapyard.

Slowly he lifted his head farther. He saw some sort of large, closed garage door at the far end of the room. Peter managed to sit up and examined his wrecked appearance. He was naked. His skin was swollen and pale from the heat. It was red only where the ropes binding his legs had left an even cable pattern. He had to cut through these ropes right now if he wanted to make it out of here. He hadn't quite finished the thought when he saw a sharp metal object in a corner of the trunk. Was that even possible? A carpet knife. It had been there all along. How many days? Why hadn't he discovered it earlier?

Trembling, he managed to kneel and turn around, to better reach the knife. It was stuck in the corner; he had to apply all his fading strength to pull it out of there with his fettered hands. Finally, he held it in his sweaty palms. He wouldn't be able to open the handcuffs with this knife, but certainly he could cut through the ropes around his legs, and the disgusting, reeking cloth tied over his mouth to keep the gag in place.

He got right to work. It was exhausting, but he freed his legs. His hands were bleeding. He had cut himself several times with the sharp blade, but he didn't feel the pain. His only thought was to escape. As fast as possible, before his tormentor returned. A sudden wave of fear swept through his wrecked body. *Hurry up, Peter! You won't get a second chance.*

.　　.　　.

The camera zoomed closer in on the man with the gag in his mouth. He'd been fumbling with those ropes for twenty minutes. His predecessor had been considerably more adept and faster. It seemed like this one here wouldn't cause any problems. What a pathetic wimp. And how it had reeked inside the trunk, every time he had opened the lid. It probably didn't stink that much in hell.

He looked closely at the screen. Still struggling. Judging from what he saw, he figured he'd have enough time left for a prayer. He got up from his chair and hummed his favorite tune while he kindled the thick, white candles on his little home altar. In a few minutes, he would liberate the world from yet another sinner. Someone who had committed a deadly sin: being rich without having worked for it. That was almost as abhorrent as buying an indulgence letter! The people had forgotten that God's warriors were still around. No sin remained unpunished, even if modern life made it easy for mankind to believe otherwise.

·   ·   ·

At long last, Peter managed to free himself from the ropes and the gag. His throat was completely dried out. Desperately—and unsuccessfully—he tried to swallow in order to at least bring some saliva to his leathery tongue. With what was left of the strength in his body, he tried to heave his numb and stiff legs out of the trunk, and he fell down hard on the tiled floor.

His knees bled. His kneecaps throbbed. Peter bit his lower lip, forcing himself to ignore the pain. *Get up and get out of here!* he told himself. With his still-fettered hands he grasped the edge of the rusty trunk and, with tremendous effort and pain, lifted himself up. *Almost!* When he finally stood upright, he looked over the car. He was inside what looked to be an abandoned car wash.

He staggered around the car and stopped abruptly when he heard a quiet humming, and then suddenly the car wash sprang to life. Peter realized that he stood right underneath one of the huge, rotating brushes. He jumped forward and stumbled over one of the small tracks on the ground. He tried to regain his balance, but his limbs were far too stiff. He slipped on the wet tiles and hit his forehead on the floor. Everything around him went black. He fought to remain conscious. One of his cheeks touched the tiles. He tried to lift his head. Metallic liquid sprayed all over, and Peter soon found himself soaked. When he finally managed to look up, he discovered something on the floor, right there where his face had been. It looked rubbery, somehow. And then he felt a delirious pain throughout his entire body. He looked down at his hands. The skin was coming off, or so it seemed. He picked up the rubbery, shredded thing on the floor. Oh dear God, it was part of his face! Panic overwhelmed him. The acid was eating into his skin. He crawled to the wall, trying to reach the garage door. The glaring light made it almost impossible to see. Then the brushes stopped, and he saw what appeared to be a white angel wafting toward him. In the palm of one hand, the angel carried a partial sun. It sparkled golden, reflecting the beams from the glaring lamps. The angel stepped up and used the half-moon-shaped blade to swiftly sever Peter's throat. Peter's red blood blended with the white and golden lights and spilled across the tiles. The last thing Peter heard was the angel singing indecipherable phrases in Latin. Then suddenly the pain was over. He was dead.

. . .

Emily hit the accelerator. It was already late, and the country road was pitch-dark. All day long her thoughts had revolved around Oliver and the lunch they had spent together. She still felt the warmth of his body. Who would have thought that she'd fall in love with a cop! The detectives she knew from TV shows seemed utterly incapable of having relationships. In fact, Emily had always imagined the average detective to be a stupid, macho womanizer who jumped from one bed to the next. She imagined how awful she would feel if it turned out that Oliver was dating her only because of a ridiculous bet between him and his colleagues. But he never made her feel like a conquest, and he was too awkward and sincere for that kind of ploy. His blue eyes conveyed pure honesty, and she felt sheltered when he looked at her. Now, just the mere thought of him brought a smile to her face.

Emily longed for a happy and lasting relationship. So far, her various attempts with very different types of men hadn't been fruitful. The most painful experience had been her affair with a married professor at her university. Like a naive little girl, she had fallen head over heels for her professor, her passionate temperament stubbornly ignoring every warning sign from the start. Eventually, despite all the promises, he had stayed with his wife and two kids. It broke Emily's heart. She would never make the same mistake again. She had become very careful before she let her guard down and allowed herself to get emotionally attached again.

Emily glanced at the glowing numerals on the dashboard clock. It was already past eleven at night. An appointment with clients had delayed Anna, who offered to postpone their meeting. But Emily really needed to speak with her tonight. It had taken them forever to find a time to get together in the first place. And besides, she had already made plans with Oliver for tomorrow.

She hit the gas again. She didn't expect a ticket at this hour. Farther ahead, she saw two alternately blinking lights. Probably malfunctioning traffic lights. But wait, those lights were green and white. When she came closer, Emily realized they were the operating lights from a car wash. *How weird,* she thought. *Isn't it too late for that?*

In any event, the nearby gas station was closed. Even the lights on the price boards were switched off. *Probably a technical error,* Emily figured, and she forgot about it as soon as she passed the car wash, continuing on to Zons. Soon she'd be at Anna's place, where a glass of red wine was already waiting for her.

.   .   .

The steel containers that seemed to scrape against the blue summer sky were enormous. Truly gigantic. Oliver was impressed. He felt like he had been taken to an alien planet. The premises of the chemical plant seemed artificial and sterile. If it hadn't been for the dry, almost copper-colored grass and the few meager trees, Oliver might not have recognized he was on Earth. Klaus stood next to him and chewed his fingernails. He always did that when he was nervous or felt overwhelmed.

Oliver wasn't surprised at all that this project had cost hundreds of millions of euros. And another thing was clear to him: you could make more than just one dead body disappear inside these huge containers.

"Good morning, detectives!"

A slick, well-groomed man in his fifties greeted them with an outstretched hand. His suntanned face was full of delicate lines and furrows, and he sported a neat mustache. An impeccably white silk handkerchief was tucked inside his left lapel pocket, and a massive signet ring glittered on one of his fingers. Oliver and Klaus were meeting with Karl Rotenburg, the PR representative of the Dormagen Chemical Works.

Oliver hesitated, then politely shook Rotenburg's hand. He couldn't stand guys like this. Back in high school he had developed a genuine distaste for posers and smart-asses clad in expensive designer garb. It was all about appearances. But Klaus didn't seem to mind—he smiled broadly at Rotenburg. Oliver almost expected him to pat the publicist's shoulder.

"If I may ask, how did you two manage to get this far on our private property?" Rotenburg's smile couldn't quite cover his disapproval.

"Oh, that was easy." Oliver took a deep breath, stuck his chest out, and said, "Your young gatekeeper was kind enough to accompany us to this point." He made an attempt to flash an artificial grin back at Rotenburg but failed. He turned his head to where he had last seen the young security guard, but, to his surprise, the guy was gone.

Rotenburg cleared his throat and pointed at various sections marked in different colors. "The areas marked in red are restricted and cannot be entered. Beneath them are the ventilation shafts for the plant. You know, unfortunately, we had a few accidents several years ago and have since upped our security measures."

"I understand. Well, you gave us some information about your employee Markus Heilkamp over the phone yesterday. Now we'd like to see where he worked. Is that possible?"

"Of course. Basically, Heilkamp was responsible for the entire plant. And he was involved in the planning of the new hydrochloric-acid tanks. For us, the acid is just a by-product. We don't process it any further. Back in the day, we simply neutralized the hydrochloric acid and disposed of it. But last year, with ever-rising financial pressures, we decided to sell it. You may have read in the newspapers that we gained an international partner. A chemical corporation from Finland has located to a nearby site and will use our acid as a flocculating agent for drinking-water purification."

"How so? Hydrochloric acid is supposed to improve the quality of potable water?" Oliver shook his head in disbelief. Acid in drinking water?

"Well, gentlemen, it's a very simple chemical reaction. Just imagine all the dirt particles in the water clinging together like flocks that can easily be fished out of the water."

Rotenburg launched into an endless lecture about flocculating agents and their role in the water-purification process. His monologue and the heat made Oliver dizzy. He didn't want to listen to this guy any longer. His thoughts were somewhere entirely different—on Emily. But Rotenburg would not let himself be dismissed so easily. When he noticed that the two detectives weren't paying attention, he raised his voice: "The new plant will be so much more eco-friendly than those old acid tanks over there." He waved his arms, trying to garner Oliver and Klaus's fullest attention. "These new tanks fulfill all the current requirements. Each tank is eighty feet high, with a diameter of about two hundred feet. They hold a volume of 194,230 cubic feet. The inner shell is made of an innovative, rubbery steel."

"This all sounds fantastic, but where did you say Heilkamp worked, again?"

"Come with me, I'll show you his office."

They walked past a sea of green, red, and blue markings on the ground until they arrived at a small, silvery construction trailer that served as a makeshift office space.

"Our new office buildings are under construction over there." Rotenburg waved an arm again. "They won't be finished for a couple of months, which is why Herr Heilkamp coordinated all pertinent activities from this trailer. Just a temporary thing."

They entered the office, which was much bigger inside than it appeared from the outside. Klaus nudged Oliver and pointed at an elderly man sitting at a desk at the far end of the trailer. Oliver nodded. They would question the man later. Naturally, direct reports and other coworkers had more helpful things to say than supervisors or publicists, for they actually knew the missing persons or victims.

"Gentlemen, take all the time you need. Over there, that's Herr Meyer, who has been filling in for Herr Heilkamp since his disappearance."

"Let's go back again to Heilkamp's last day here. What exactly did you do that day?"

"You know, I'd have to say nothing out of the ordinary. As you can see for yourselves, the construction of the new acid tanks has been completed. All that was left was to coordinate the distribution of the acid and set up the maintenance of the tanks. We had a good thousand gallons of hydrochloric acid delivered to several clients that day."

Rotenburg pulled a green binder from one of the shelves and showed it to Oliver and Klaus. "Look here, everything has been meticulously recorded. These are the complete delivery slips from this year. Again, please take all the time you need to study everything. Markus Heilkamp was an excellent employee, and we miss him dearly. We'd like to have him back as soon as possible."

Oliver leafed through the binder with its overwhelming stack of delivery slips. Clearly, the hydrochloric-acid business was lucrative. At first glance, everything looked level. Oliver wrote down the names of the companies that had received hydrochloric acid during the two weeks prior to Heilkamp's disappearance. The delivery volumes were always enormous. It seemed rather improbable that the killer or killers would have acquired the acid directly from this plant. And the detectives didn't know yet whether Heilkamp was even dead. But maybe the killers had secretly managed to siphon off a small amount of acid.

"The remaining amount inside the tanks is measured and inspected on a regular basis, that's what you said, Herr Rotenburg?"

"Yes, of course. We keep track of every single drop. It's the law. We're also obligated to ensure that the tanks are leakproof. With that aggressive an acid, we need to be extra cautious. We meet the highest safety standards, but there's always a big risk of leakage, especially around the welding seams. That's why we routinely check the volume inside the tanks."

"Would you mind us speaking with Herr Heilkamp's replacement for a minute? Remind me of his name again?"

"Meyer, Herr Meyer. Of course." Rotenburg called over the man at the desk.

"Herr Meyer, these are detectives Oliver Bergmann and Klaus Gruber. They're investigating Herr Heilkamp's disappearance. Please give them all the information they need."

Herr Meyer blushed. He couldn't meet Oliver's gaze and lowered his eyes while he greeted Oliver with a slack handshake.

"Did you know Herr Heilkamp well?" Oliver asked. "Did you hang out, outside of work?"

Herr Meyer's voice was unusually high-pitched and brittle. "We did. I went to his place often. He owns a little farmhouse near Zons. He was feeling quite lonely since his divorce, and we often sat together over a few beers. I got divorced two years before him. We had a lot to share."

"Did he have any special plans on the night he went missing?"

"No, he was very tired throughout the day and wanted to rest. He'd been on a blind date the night before, with a pretty brunette." Meyer grinned, and for a moment, his hollow cheeks looked rosy and healthy. After an embarrassed glance over to Rotenburg, he stared at the ground again.

"Do you know the name of the lady?"

"He showed me her profile. Her alias was Wild Bee."

"And you don't know her real name?"

"Her first name is Sabine. I didn't ask her last name. He might not even know it. And it didn't seem that important. He's been doing quite a bit of online dating. He really wanted a new beginning after his divorce."

"Was he planning on meeting Sabine again?"

"Yes, he would usually go on a second date. He used to say he liked taking a closer look the second time around. I think you understand what I mean."

Oliver nodded. He had heard enough for now. The information was interesting, but he didn't think the murderer was a woman. If Markus Heilkamp even was the victim they were looking for. At this point he was only missing, and they didn't know if the bones were his.

"Does the company exploit all the by-products, or do you also store unusable residues?"

"You're referring to what we call our residue cemetery? That's where we deposit everything that can't be used or processed. We also store replacement parts there. It's a little more than two miles from here, at the far end of the premises. Would you like to take a look?"

"Maybe another time. Thank you very much. You helped us a lot today."

Rotenburg walked them to the gate. After a short good-bye, Oliver and Klaus drove back to the precinct. Their next stop would be Markus Heilkamp's farmhouse, where they hoped to gather some DNA that could help them determine whether or not the bones were his.

.   .   .

He had seen them coming yesterday, the two tall detectives. One of them looked exactly like he'd always imagined a detective would look. Tight, faded jeans; brown boots; and a worn-out T-shirt that emphasized his well-toned chest and muscular arms. His dark hair was ruffled, and his black eyebrows framed his bright-blue eyes. His chiseled face was tanned, and he moved with a smooth strength that called to mind a tiger on the hunt. The other guy wasn't that interesting. He was much older and evidently didn't work out as much as his partner. He could have passed as the younger one's father, had it not been for his completely different eyes. Grayish blue, they seemed friendly and somehow harmless. Those were not the eyes of a hunter. He had learned as much from his master by now.

Because he often helped out at the gate of Dormagen Chemical Works, following the two detectives hadn't been complicated at all. His master was very proud of him yesterday when he reported, during their online chat session, that the two men would return the following day. How fast his heart had pounded when he'd left his position at the gate without permission and guided the detectives as near to the acid tanks as possible. How close they were to the danger-zone markings, and they didn't have a clue! If his master had not expressly forbidden it, he surely would have surrendered to temptation and made the detectives disappear in one of those large underground tanks. Or at least one of the detectives.

Why did they have to show up and sniff around? He hadn't done anything wrong. Not since he had last served time. And that sentence hadn't even been justified. He had done nothing to that woman—he had only wanted to touch her, not hit her, let alone kill her! Touching wasn't illegal, was it? He hadn't treated her as bad as that bitch had claimed in court. Next time he'd be more careful when choosing a woman.

But now was not the time. For now, he had to focus on these two detectives and find out their next moves. How convenient, that they'd been so impressed by those hydrochloric-acid tanks! They hadn't even noticed when he hid behind the wall of a nearby building. He had known to make himself almost invisible and stayed on their heels. He even returned on time to his post at the gate. Perfectly inconspicuous. Just like his master had taught him.

. . .

The alarm clock's jarring ring was merciless. With her eyes closed, Anna felt for the clock on her nightstand. It took forever before she finally found the button. She let out a deep sigh and sank back into her pillow. The night couldn't possibly be over yet. But the sunlight flickering playfully through the blinds said otherwise. Anna pulled the duvet over her head. There was no way she could get up. Her head was throbbing. Her entire body screamed. She let out another deep breath and, from under the cover, glanced at Emily, who was sleeping peacefully. Oh, those blessed students who could sleep anywhere, anytime, no matter how much noise was around them.

Anna rubbed her eyes. After three years with the bank, she still hadn't adjusted to the rhythm. Getting up early remained a torture. Of course, emptying many glasses of red wine with Emily last night and staying up long hours in front of the computer, doing research for Emily's new feature about another medieval serial killer in Zons, made it even harder. Her brain was mush.

Plus, she'd had such an intense dream. This often happened when she drank too much. Usually, when she dreamt of Bastian Mühlenberg, she would see an oil painting of him and his wife, Marie. Over and over she'd experience that deep sense of confusion that had first invaded her when she learned there was no Bastian Mühlenberg alive today. In those dreams, she relived every single encounter they'd had, especially their last one. That was the night when he insisted Anna come meet him at the Miller's Tower, thus keeping her from going home to her apartment, where a killer was waiting for her.

Since that night, she hadn't seen Bastian Mühlenberg again. And last night's dream had been different from the others. This time she clearly saw Bastian in the past. It was a multilayered dream—fast, dark, and dangerous. Anna saw Bastian hurry through countless dark alleys. He was gathering silver keys and stringing them on a necklace. Then she saw a fatally ill man lying in bed. He very much resembled Bastian. Bastian sat by the man's bedside, looking sad and holding the sick man's hand. He shook his head in disbelief, and his blond hair swayed.

Then she saw Bastian open a big, old, ornate treasure chest with one of the silver keys. The image became blurry and vanished. The next thing Anna saw was a map with cryptic symbols. Seconds later, she found herself inside a dark vault. Her heart was pounding fast and she was paralyzed with fear because she knew she had lost her way. The vault turned out to be a maze with thousands of dark hallways, all damp and dirty. Vermin crawled over her feet. Just when she couldn't take it anymore, there was Bastian, clutching a torch, and then the two of them were having a picnic on the sunny banks of the Rhine. She remembered how he had looked at her with his brown eyes. He leaned over to her, so close that she could feel his warm breath on her cheeks. She longed to kiss him, but Bastian wanted to whisper something in her ear first. Anna heard the words, but they didn't make any sense.

Then the jarring, merciless sound of the alarm tore her out of the one beautiful moment in that entire dream. Anna pressed her hands against her head. She desperately needed an Advil. Or two. Her cell phone rang.

No! Not Matthias Kronberg again! That guy really wore on her nerves. She finally rolled out of bed. On her way into the kitchen, she answered the call.

"Yes?"

"Good morning, Frau Winterfeld. I hope I'm not disturbing you. I'm sorry to bother you again, but I really need to know if I'll get that loan."

Anna had to think for a moment. What exactly was the issue here? What had her boss told her? She knew they had spoken about it. Then she remembered.

"Herr Kronberg, please don't worry. Everything's under way. I still need to hear back from our Risk Management Department, but I believe everything will be fine. Can I call you back later?"

Kronberg sounded disappointed. "All right. Promise you'll let me know as soon as you have word. Please."

Anna agreed and hung up. In the bathroom, she took two Advil without water, walked back into the bedroom, and tenderly stroked Emily's hair.

"Hey, sleepyhead, wake up!"

Emily rubbed her eyes.

"Emily, I'm off to work. There's breakfast and coffee in the kitchen. I've put the printouts about the killer with the golden sickle on top of your bag so you won't forget them. Call me later and tell me all about your date with Oliver," Anna told her sleepy friend with a smile. *Those two really have a nice romance going on,* she thought. How she wished she could have that, too, for once. "And in case you need some Advil, here." She put the bottle on the pillow next to Emily.

"Are you really sure the story about the killer with the sickle is a good one?" Emily's voice was drowsy and hoarse.

"Of course. It'll be your next big piece, the perfect sequel to your features about the fatal puzzle. You've got almost everything together already. Some more research at the county archive, and that's it. You're a great writer; of course you can do it!"

And the best thing about this one is that the killer with the golden sickle has nothing to do with me, Anna mused.

Or does he? A sinister thought rushed through her mind, and for a brief moment, she saw the image of a golden sickle flare up inside a dark vault. The image gave her goose bumps. The hair on her arms immediately stood up, and a cold shiver ran down her spine. *Calm down, you're overreacting because you had a bad dream,* she told herself. Pushing the dark thoughts aside, she grabbed her car keys and headed to work.

IX
Five Hundred Years Ago

In his dreams, Bastian saw that beautiful woman again. He tossed and turned in his sleep. The woman had skin as white as edelweiss and large, emerald eyes. Her long curls framed her white neck and flowed gently over her shoulders, down to her slender waist. He knew that woman. He just couldn't remember where he had met her. Her wonderful eyes were filled with fear. Why?

He came a step closer. The look in her eyes changed. She beamed at him, and his heart jumped with joy. He wanted to touch her, but some invisible power held him back. Then she moved away from him, and her image turned blurry. He looked for her. Where could she be? He ran through a maze of dark, vault-like alleys until he was sure he would never find his way back out. But then there she was, up ahead at the end of the alley. Bastian ran toward her. A sudden ray of light cut across the alley, and abruptly he was in a different world. It was daylight. He and the beautiful woman were sitting on the banks of the Rhine. Her lips were so red and close. He could smell her sweet perfume.

Bastian woke up not knowing where he was. He looked around. Slowly, his eyes adjusted to the darkness. He was in his familiar, modest bedroom. Marie was lying next to him, breathing peace-fully. The moonlight shone on her pretty face, and her hair glittered like gold. He looked over to the window. A full moon was up in the sky. That explained the strange, haunting dream. On full-moon nights, Zons's most recent serial killer, obsessed with divine delu-sions, had viciously murdered the victims of his fatal puzzle.

Bastian took a deep breath. That danger was over. He thought again of the fearful young woman from his dream. He didn't know exactly who she was, but he was sure he had seen her several times before. But how was that possible? Was he going crazy?

He slipped out from underneath the covers and quietly sneaked downstairs to the kitchen. He rinsed his sweat-soaked face in a bucket of water. What a treat! His mind became clear, and he could feel the veil of drowsiness lifting.

Bring me the third key! Father Johannes's words still echoed in his head. Bastian thought about how he could possibly fulfill the priest's wish. The Fraternity of Saint Sebastian scared him. Not that Bastian wasn't a pious man. Of course he was. Bastian had spent half his life in the company of Father Johannes, inside his church. To Bastian, the priest emanated a warm, bright light, and he could hear God's mercy through Father Johannes's words. But Huppertz Helpenstein was a completely different story. Each of his words seemed sinister and cold. Instead of kindness and forgive-ness, he exuded menace and punishment. The other members of the fraternity seemed timid and diffident. There was not much left of the pride that had once distinguished those bold fighters who had so courageously helped liberate the besieged city of Neuss. Bastian thought of this every time he saw the brothers kneel down at the Saint Sebastianus altar that Huppertz had donated.

For a brief moment, Bastian considered slipping back into bed next to Marie, but he decided otherwise. He wouldn't be able to fall asleep again anyway. So he quickly got dressed in his pants and jerkin and slid out of the house. It was far too early to speak with Wernhart, but he figured they might be able to find the third key together. After all, Wernhart seemed to know a lot about the keys and that treasure chest. At least, he knew more about it than Bastian.

Bastian walked a few steps and paused in front of his father's mill. In the moonlight, the Miller's Tower looked formidable. The sails of the mill creaked in the breeze. It was a familiar, dear sound to Bastian, the sound of home. The mill functioned as the southwestern cornerstone of the city wall. The wall itself was enormous—forty feet high, built of basaltic rock, and, to this day, no enemy had been able to conquer the solid fortification. It had been built according to the latest architectural standards, and Bastian's entire family took great pride in the fact that their mill was an integral part of the whole construction.

On a whim, Bastian decided to go to Huppertz Helpenstein's house. He didn't expect much of this visit but hoped he might come up with more ideas along the way. He walked stealthily on the cobblestone streets to avoid unnecessary noise. Huppertz lived on the easternmost edge of the fortified city, on Mauerstraße—Wall Street. His house almost bordered the *Zollturm*, the Customs Tower. It was a popular and coveted residential area, as it was close to the customs office and offered easy access to the Rhine meadows and the river.

Bastian hurried through his peacefully sleeping hometown. Even the rats that usually liked to rush through the darkness seemed to be asleep. Yet from inside old Jacob's house came a sound. Bastian stopped and listened to his snoring. Good old Jacob, who always claimed he couldn't close his eyes at night for all his worries, was about to make the few shingles left on his humble roof fall to the street with his snores. Bastian smiled, then continued on.

At the corner of the next square, Hospitalplatz, he stopped again and listened carefully. This time, no snoring interrupted the silence. He stuck his head around the corner and peeked into Mauerstraße.

He vaguely recognized the silhouette of Huppertz Helpenstein's house at the far end of the small street. Bastian tiptoed closer. Just as he was about to cross the street to the other side, he noticed a movement in front of Huppertz's house. A black figure jumped away from the dark facade and disappeared around the corner, onto Rheinstraße. The echoes of the steps sounded like crunching pebbles, and then they faded in the darkness. Bastian held his breath. Had that really happened?

Not a minute went by and then a second dark figure left the house and disappeared in the same direction. That couldn't possibly be. What was the fraternity's business here in the middle of the night? Bastian's senses were on high alert. He sneaked as close to the door as he could get, hearing muffled voices inside yet unable to understand the words. He pressed his ear against the wall, which didn't help.

Then he noticed a window that was open a crack, but all he could see was the weak light of a candle. Suddenly, the door opened again. Bastian pressed his body against the wall and covered his blond hair with the hood of his jerkin.

"Please express my heartfelt condolences to Benedict Eschenbach's family. He was a great standard-bearer, and we will hold his memory in the highest esteem. Up until the last minute of his life, Benedict tried to keep the key safe."

Bastian recognized the voice of Gottfried, a member of the fraternity. Why would they hold nocturnal meetings at Helpenstein's home? Bastian heard the door being locked and bolted. He peeked again through the window. This time, he caught a glimpse of Huppertz Helpenstein. The fraternity master blew out the candle, making everything pitch-black. Then Bastian heard the sound of creaking floorboards. He assumed Helpenstein was retiring to his bedroom. After a while, silence had settled in again. Bastian waited a moment longer before he quietly walked home. Suddenly he was very tired and wanted to get to bed as fast as possible.

Silent as a cat, he opened his door, tiptoed up the stairs, and slipped under the covers. Marie was still sound asleep. She probably hadn't even noticed his absence. Bastian brooded over the secret meeting he had just witnessed, but after a few minutes he fell into a troubled, shallow sleep. This time, he didn't dream at all.

·   ·   ·

Bastian went to seek Wernhart's advice first thing in the morning. He sat on Wernhart's straw bed with his legs stretched out. His best friend frowned and paced up and down his small room. It was so narrow that he had to step over Bastian's feet every time he reached the middle of the room. Bastian's gaze intently followed Wernhart's pacing, and he started feeling dizzy.

"Why would they meet in the middle of the night?" Wernhart said. "Everyone knows the fraternity. They might as well gather in daylight, nobody would find that suspicious."

"I have no clue, either," Bastian said and shrugged. He couldn't wrap his head around it.

"Maybe we should check if they're meeting again tonight?"

"That's a good idea. Let's take turns each night."

"My father told me in confidence that Huppertz Helpenstein is known to wear the third key around his neck at all times. Though I'm not sure if that's really true, because a week ago, I came to visit with the doctor, Josef Hesemann, when Huppertz was leaving, and guess what I found out, Bastian!" Wernhart's eyes sparkled with excitement. He interrupted his pacing, eager to let Bastian in on the news. "Huppertz suffers from a skin condition. Hesemann has explicitly told him to take off the necklace at night—otherwise the rash might fester and develop into ulcers."

"And how do you know that?" Bastian asked, surprised.

"I eavesdropped." Embarrassed, Wernhart looked at the floor.

Bastian jumped up from the straw bed, happily patted Wernhart's shoulder, and winked. "Well, my friend, I'm sure Father Johannes will be glad to hear your confession about this!"

They grinned at each other.

At last, Bastian knew what they had to do: sneak into the fraternity master's house at night and steal the key. But before that, he and Wernhart needed to find out what time Helpenstein usually went to bed. Tonight, Wernhart would take up his post, and early tomorrow morning they would plot out how to gain possession of the third key. Bastian was exhilarated. Yet didn't this all seem too easy? Suddenly, doubts were creeping up inside him. Maybe they had overlooked some major detail?

He pushed aside the doubts and went to see Father Johannes. With luck, he'd run into Brother Ignatius in the church. Suddenly, he thought of Heinrich. He remembered how haggard and gray he had looked, and how hollow his cheeks had been. He hoped it would still be a long time until he'd have to fulfill his brother's last wish, but a sad voice inside his head whispered the bitter truth. Bastian felt an iron fist clenching around his heart: he knew that his brother didn't have much time left.

When he turned into the next alley, he saw a blonde woman walking in front of him. Her long hair was in two thick braids, and her gown fell fluidly around her hips and swept the ground as she walked. A pleased smile came to Bastian's face, and he sneaked up behind the woman. The baked goods in her basket smelled delicious. Bastian's stomach growled, and for an instant he was so distracted that he almost stepped on her dress. He jumped forward, turned around, and kissed her rosy cheeks while he reached for one of the tasty pastries in her basket.

Marie stopped and let out a cry. Bastian grinned at her and playfully bowed his head as if in shame.

"You scoundrel! Why do you scare me so?" Marie tried to hit him with her scarf. But Bastian had anticipated this move and grabbed the scarf in midair. He wrapped his arms around her hips, lifted her up, and spun her around. When he put her down again, his warm lips caressed her neck. Marie's expression softened, and she smiled.

"I'll see you as soon as I've spoken with Father Johannes," Bastian whispered in her ear. Then he hurried down the alley and out of sight as Marie gazed after him, enraptured.

.   .   .

"Of course I'll do this favor for you," said Brother Ignatius and put his large palm on Bastian's shoulder. "I'm very fond of Brother Albrecht and care about everyone who's close to him. Don't worry any longer. I know he will be there for Heinrich and give him all the comfort he needs. He will accompany him on his last journey on this Earth when the time arises. Nobody should go on that journey alone." He quickly crossed himself and gave Bastian a compassionate look.

The intensity in Brother Ignatius's eyes made Bastian shiver. Until now, he had noticed only the resemblance between the priest Johannes and his brother, Ignatius the monk. For the first time, Bastian looked deep into Ignatius's blue eyes and saw more than the kindness of a clergyman. Although he was much younger than Father Johannes, his eyes seemed very old, almost as if they had seen too much evil in this world. Benevolence alternated with harshness and back again. Bastian took another look at Ignatius. He was slender, almost as tall as Bastian, and his body seemed sinewy and wiry. They took a few steps toward the altar, and it seemed as if Ignatius were floating, with such smooth and elegant movements. Yet in contrast, his hands were rugged and swollen. Why would a monk have the hands of a farmer? Bastian didn't understand. Besides praying and maybe writing, what else did a monk do with his hands all day?

Father Johannes approached them in a hurry. Mass was about to start and he wasn't finished preparing. Bastian observed the two brothers standing next to each other. Johannes was significantly smaller than Ignatius, but the two men had similar facial features and the same gray hair.

"You haven't forgotten about the favor I asked you, dear Bastian?"

Bastian smiled and bowed. "It is constantly on my mind, Father Johannes. Rest assured that I'm about to fulfill your wish. Expect to hear from me soon."

For a moment, confusion sparked up in Ignatius's eyes, but he quickly gained control of his expression and managed a compassionate look. The first congregants entered the church, and the room was soon filled with the echo of whispers as the numbers of the faithful grew rapidly. It wasn't long before every seat was taken. The two clergymen walked up to the altar, and Bastian squeezed in next to Wernhart, who was sitting on one of the benches in the back.

. . .

She had no clue where she was. She was in terrible pain, but she was so weak that she couldn't determine where exactly the pain was coming from. She didn't even remember her own name. All she knew was that she didn't belong here, in this dark place, full of pain. How did she get here? Suddenly, the name *Jacob* rushed through her confused brain. Her husband.

It was frigid. Water dripped from the walls, creating a thousandfold echo inside the sinister vault. The steady *drip drip* rhythm produced a torturing headache. She wanted to voice her desperation and scream, but her throat produced only rattling sounds. Tears streamed down her cheeks.

For a few seconds, her mind cleared, and she relived the horrible moment when that terrible creature had cut her tongue out of her throat with a golden sickle. Instantly, she tasted the blood again. Her stomach revolted and cramped.

The nails on the wooden chair cut deeper into her sore flesh. Then, everything turned dark, her head drooped to her chest, and she blacked out. Fainting granted her a short interlude of relief.

A slender figure smoothly moved away from the damp stone walls and approached the slumped woman. With one hand, the figure pushed the woman's head to the side. Then, moving with silent grace, he left the cold vault.

.   .   .

A bright moon hovered in the sky, but the shadows between the low, closely spaced houses were so black that Wernhart had to move very slowly. He stretched out an arm and blinked. It was so dark he couldn't see his hand. Fear crept up inside him, and he felt a big lump in his throat. For a brief moment he considered turning around and going straight back to his straw bed. But he didn't want to disappoint Bastian by letting fear get the better of him. He had promised he would help. And it had been his idea to begin with. He gathered all his courage and continued to the fraternity master's house.

Wernhart took a deep breath and reached under his jerkin to feel for his dagger. It was in its place. Knowing that he carried a sharp weapon reassured him. He tiptoed along Rheinstraße in the direction of the Customs Tower. He tried to stay close to the facades of the houses on the dark side of the street. Otherwise everyone would recognize him. In case the Saint Sebastian brothers did indeed convene again this night, they'd inevitably be coming toward him from the other end of Rheinstraße, just like Bastian had observed during his reconnaissance mission the previous night. Under no circumstances must they notice him! Who knew what those sinister fellows might do to him? He imagined himself surrounded by a group of chanting men wrapped in dark cloaks with black, swaying hoods, their evil, demonic stares stabbing him without mercy. He quickly chased away the disturbing thoughts. If he didn't stop terrorizing himself, he'd probably suffer a heart attack.

Wernhart realized that walking up Rheinstraße might not be the best idea and changed plans. He would take a short detour and approach the house from the direction Bastian had chosen yesterday. That way he would avoid running into them. He turned around. His new route brought him past Schlossplatz. The square in the heart of the town was deserted. The rustling of the leaves on the trees intensified, and the trees looked as if they were performing a mysterious dance. It almost sounded like voices straying through the night. Wernhart shivered but bravely continued on, always making sure he didn't step outside the protection of the shadows cast from the eaves of the houses.

A sudden clattering behind him scared Wernhart half to death. What was that? The Devil riding through the night? Wernhart pictured himself lying on the curb, trampled to death by the hooves of a black horse. *Only some shutters clattering in the wind,* he realized after the shock wore off.

He took another deep breath and turned into the alley that led to Huppertz's house. In the distance, he heard the echo of footsteps coming closer. Someone was approaching. Oh dear God, they had discovered him! Panic took hold of him, and he pressed his shaking body against the facade as if he might dissolve into the stone wall. He felt under his jerkin for his dagger.

As the person came closer, Wernhart recognized the flickering light of a candle. Why was this person carrying a lantern? Then he knew. It was only Bechtolt, the night watchman. He turned into the next alley, and Wernhart hurried along. He was running now, still trying to stay within the shadows. Just a few feet separated him from the house. What was waiting for him there?

Darkness and silence. Not even the night wind managed to intrude on the stillness. A black, heavy gown of silence wrapped around the Helpenstein residence. All Wernhart could hear was his own frenetic panting and his wildly pounding heart.

He sneaked up to a window and squatted directly underneath. He decided he'd stay for a while. Who knew what this adventure might have in store? He waited. And waited. Soon, his limbs were so stiff they hurt, but nothing had happened. It was just dark and quiet.

Wernhart rose to his feet. He could feel the blood rushing back into his legs. The bottoms of his feet tingled as if a thousand little needles were poking them. He shifted his weight back and forth until it didn't hurt anymore. Then he felt along the window frame. To his surprise, the window was ajar. He pushed it open and stared into the dark, silent room.

He heaved himself over the windowsill. Now he was inside Huppertz's house. He ducked down and remained quiet. He couldn't hear anything and felt his way through the darkness. Where would Huppertz most likely keep his necklace at night? Probably next to his bed. Wernhart moaned quietly. Should he really dare to walk up the stairs and sneak into Huppertz's bedroom? What if he woke up?

He didn't waste a second thought. Silver rays of moonlight fell through the more elevated windows on the first floor, and when Wernhart reached the top of the stairs, his vision improved. He could discern the shapes of the few pieces of furniture and found himself in a small room with only a closet and a wooden chair. A black cloth was draped over the chair, and two clunky, clog-like wooden shoes sat in front of the closet. He turned around and banged against a metal washtub filled with water. Thankfully, the tub didn't fall over, but the water inside sloshed heavily. For a second, Wernhart stopped breathing and froze. What if someone heard the noise? Then he saw another, smaller container, right next to the washtub. This one was filled with something sparkling. Wernhart bent down to take a closer look. Coins! He took one and brought it up to his eyes. These were real gold coins! Where did Huppertz get all this money? He quietly put the gulden back. From the adjacent room came a creaking noise. Then everything was silent again. The door to that other room had been left ajar. Wernhart peeked through the small gap.

The moonlight was particularly bright in this room, and Wernhart recognized the fraternity master and his wife in bed. They were sound asleep. A linen sheet covered half of Huppertz's face and moved slowly up and down to the rhythm of his snoring, but that was the only movement. Wernhart felt queasy with fear. But he hadn't come this far to give up now! He tiptoed toward the bed.

His pulse quickened when he spotted the necklace with the silver key lying on the nightstand. Almost there! With trembling fingers, he reached for the precious object. In his hurry, he accidentally stumbled against the bedpost and stood paralyzed. Huppertz opened his eyes wide. His eye sockets were deep and dark. For a few seconds, both men stared at each other, but Huppertz composed himself faster and jumped out of bed. His wife screamed. The peace of the night had been broken. Wernhart ran down the stairs as fast as his legs would take him, Huppertz's stomping feet close behind. The fraternity master was quicker than Wernhart had expected. Huppertz grabbed the back of Wernhart's jerkin, but in a tremendous act of will and effort, Wernhart pulled away. Still, it was too late. He felt something wooden smack his head hard. Light exploded in front of his eyes. *Save the key!* That was his last thought before he tumbled down the stairs and hit the floor. In his last conscious act, he shoved the small key and slender chain into his mouth and swallowed with all his might. He tried not to cough up his treasure right away; it wasn't easy. But before he passed out, he felt the key and necklace slowly gliding down his esophagus.

. . .

"We can't just hand him over to the City Guard! He saw the gold coins!" Huppertz snapped at Wilhelm, his fellow fraternity brother. Wilhelm quickly took a step back.

"Let's keep him here until we come up with a better plan."

"Are you sure he stole the key?"

"Who else, you fool? I know for a fact that I still had the key yesterday evening."

"That was the last key. What should we do now?"

"Calm down, Wilhelm. It will resurface, sooner or later. I'm confident."

"What if someone opens the chest?"

"Now you listen to me. Even if someone were to succeed in bringing all three keys into his possession, that still doesn't tell him where the chest is!"

Huppertz locked the small, damp room in the cellar. That oaf Wernhart wouldn't be able to escape, that much was certain. And he would tell where he had hidden the key. Huppertz would take care of that—forcibly, if necessary. Huppertz shoved Wilhelm up the stairs.

At first, Huppertz had thought Wernhart had lost the key when he tumbled down the stairs. But he had combed the entire house several times and could not find it. That bastard. Once Huppertz got the key back, he would silence Wernhart forever. He shouldn't have seen the gold coins. He definitely knew too much.

. . .

An uneasy feeling came over Bastian. He should never have let Wernhart go to Huppertz's house alone. His friend should have been back some time ago, and Bastian had an inkling that Wernhart wasn't coming back at all. Oh dear God, what should he do? Wait for the night and then try to go on a rescue mission? *No, don't be foolish, Bastian,* he scolded himself. *In the darkness, they'll easily snatch you away as well.*

He would have to try to rescue his friend in broad daylight. Nobody would be prepared for such a bold move. But how? Should he just walk into Huppertz's house? The street was busy during the day, and the house was very close to the Customs Tower. But that might be an advantage. Amid the crowd around the customs office, he wouldn't arouse any suspicion.

The next morning, pulling a cart that he had borrowed from the mill, he set off to rescue his friend. Usually, the cart was used for transporting bags of flour, but today, its bed was empty. A thick linen cloth protected it from the curious glances of onlookers. He couldn't stop thinking about Wernhart. He would never forgive himself if something had happened to him. Suddenly he felt a wave of despair. He pictured Huppertz's evil eyes. He didn't need much imagination to conjure up what this man was capable of. He saw poor Wernhart lying on the floor of a cold dungeon. He was bound, and men clad in black cloaks, their hoods drawn, formed a circle around him. They chanted an eerie melody, and then one of them lifted a red-hot iron pole and was about to jab it right into

Wernhart's heart . . . Bastian took a deep breath and tried to chase away the frightening vision.

Only one night had passed since they had captured Wernhart. It wasn't too late yet. He turned onto Mauerstraße. Just as he had expected, a colorful, boisterous crowd was going about their business, and nobody paid attention to Bastian when he stopped in front of Huppertz's house, focused for a second, and boldly walked through the open door. After three large steps, he stood in the middle of the living room and, with his heart beating wildly, tried to make up his mind. Where should he look first? His glance fell on a small wooden door underneath the staircase, and he tiptoed toward it. He heard Huppertz's wife puttering around in the kitchen and was extra careful.

The wooden door looked small, but it was very heavy, and Bastian had trouble opening it. He feared it would squeak so loudly that everyone would hear it. Yet when it finally swung open, it didn't make a sound.

Bastian's heart was pounding in his ears. Panic gripped him. He had never sneaked into someone's house before. His senses were on full alert. From somewhere in the cellar came a muffled moaning. He tiptoed down the wet, slippery stone stairs. At one point he almost fell but managed to regain his balance.

The air smelled damp and musty. He stepped into a puddle, and water soaked his shoes, a reminder of the recent flood. Because Zons was located so close to the Rhine, floods were common, and most cellars were usually damp, especially those closer to the meadows. In the utter darkness, he slowly walked to the left, since the moaning seemed to be coming from that direction. He let his fingers run along the damp wall. When he suddenly encountered something wooden, Bastian tensed up. A door—to a shed, maybe? Had he discovered Wernhart's cell? He felt across the wooden surface until he recognized a massive iron chain with a padlock. Swiftly, he pulled out the iron tong he'd been carrying under his jerkin and set to work. *Clack!* The lock opened. The chain banged against the wooden door, and the sound echoed from the walls.

"Wernhart, is that you in there?" Bastian whispered. The moaning continued, but he didn't hear an answer. He opened the door just wide enough to slip through. A sudden draft made the door slam shut with a loud bang. Bastian froze in panic. Within a few seconds, he heard heavy steps coming hastily down the stairs. He held his breath.

Light flickered through the cracks of the wooden door. Pressed against a dark corner, Bastian braced himself to attack. His nerves were almost impossible to control. He would be discovered any second. But the light didn't come closer.

He heard a man say, "False alarm" in a low, gruff voice. The man's steps quickly faded. Then Bastian heard the upper door close. His heart raced and his face was drenched in sweat. Panting and with shaking hands, he leaned his head against the cool stones of the wall. That was close!

Then he heard the moaning again. It came from the other end of the room. Carefully, Bastian crawled across the damp floor, feeling his way with his hands. Wet, rotting straw clung to his fingers. Then his hand hit something leather. A shoe! Excited, Bastian continued to feel around in the darkness. Someone was lying here. *Wernhart?* There it was again, the quiet moaning. Bastian put a hand on the whimpering man's shoulder and gently shook him.

"Wernhart, is that you? Say something, please."

Nothing. The man kept moaning. Bastian touched the back of the man's head and felt a sticky liquid. It was blood. The poor fellow must have a bad head wound. Judging from the hair, Bastian was quite certain he had found his friend. He strained his muscles and heaved the heavy body onto his broad shoulders. He weighed as much as two flour bags, if not more, but being a miller's son,

Bastian had carried heavier loads. Slowly, he moved over the slippery ground. At the bottom of the stairs he paused and listened carefully. Upstairs it was silent. Were they waiting to ambush him? He had no choice. He recalled the layout of the living room upstairs. In five fast steps he could be out on the street, safe. They wouldn't dare attack him outside. Everybody knew he belonged to the City Guard, and he was sure Huppertz wouldn't drag him back inside in view of everyone.

Bastian's heart hammered against his ribs. He took a deep breath and focused on his task. He knew he could do it. Step after step he moved up the stairs, avoiding the dangerous uneven areas he remembered from the way down. When he reached the last step, he paused. The wounded man moaned.

With no time to waste, Bastian pushed against the heavy door and opened it a crack. It took his eyes a while to get used to the bright light. The room was empty, or so it seemed. The hammering of a nearby blacksmith was nothing against the sound of Bastian's heart. Sweat streamed down his face. He wouldn't be able to carry his friend for very much longer. It was now or never.

He opened the door wide. There was no one around. Bastian hurried through the room, out the door, and across the street to his cart. A woman witnessed his escape and stared at him in shock, but Bastian ignored her. He quickly laid the man on the truck bed—thank God, it was, indeed, Wernhart—and covered him with the linen. Then he left Mauerstraße as fast as he could. His friend had bled profusely and needed immediate medical care. Bastian had to find the doctor, Josef Hesemann, right away.

. . .

Wernhart's breathing was shallow, but he was alive and had come to. He was slumped on a chair in front of Bastian and Josef. Both men looked at him with deep concern.

Wheezing and rattling, Wernhart filled them in on his nocturnal adventure in Huppertz's house, including the most important fact, that he had swallowed the key and the necklace. *What a smart idea,* Bastian thought, *to do just like the standard-bearer Benedict Eschenbach had done—though Wernhart could easily have injured his pharynx.*

With two wooden brackets placed between Wernhart's upper and lower jaw, Josef opened Wernhart's mouth as wide as possible and carefully reached inside his pharynx. It made Wernhart gag and he turned his head to the side.

"Hold still now, will you!" Josef looked sternly at his patient. Wernhart surrendered and leaned his head back.

"Bastian, hold his head tightly as best you can. The necklace has slid pretty far down, and I'm afraid we won't be able to get it out this way."

Josef frowned and gave it another try. But the necklace slipped from his fingers. When he tried again, with a linen cloth wrapped around his fingers, he got hold of it. He managed to pull the object a few fractions of an inch out of Wernhart's esophagus, but gave up when he sensed resistance. It was too dangerous. If he ripped open the esophagus tissue, Wernhart would be dead in no time. It wouldn't be the first time Josef had seen someone destroyed by his own gastric acid.

"Bastian, we need to find another way to get this out. Bring me a large bucket full of water." Josef walked over to the medicine cabinet and pulled out a bottle of castor oil. He poured a substantial spoonful into a wooden bowl.

"Drink this, Wernhart. This bucket of water should get you through the evening. Please relieve yourself over there in the corner and make sure everything goes into the respective container. If we're lucky, we might see the key and necklace very soon."

"I trust you won't speak to anyone about this?" Bastian looked at the doctor.

"I shall speak neither a word about the key and chain we found in poor Benedict's pharynx, nor about the one that will hopefully exit Wernhart's intestines any minute. Rest assured, my dear Bastian."

They were interrupted by a cry of agony and turned around. Wernhart was crouching on the floor in terrible pain. Both arms clasped around his stomach, he hustled over to his designated corner. Josef was right: the key was about to reappear!

X
Present

The heat in the tiny, sticky space was unbearable. Terrible cramps gripped her stomach and almost made her faint. She forced herself to swallow down the disgusting acid that kept coming up in her throat. She must not throw up. She took a deep breath. It was hot and dark. The light that fell through a small crack in her prison was not enough to help her find her bearings. She had the feeling she was caught inside the trunk of a car, but she wasn't sure. "You don't have any idea where you are," she muttered to herself. Another violent cramp shook her, and this time she vomited uncontrollably. Immediately she smelled the sour odor around her. She tried to turn her head to the side, but it didn't work. Her arms and legs were tightly bound and she couldn't move an inch.

Exhausted, she let her head drop down, and her cheek landed in her own vomit. Tortured sobs escaped her aching throat, and thick tears ran down her face. *Pull yourself together! Save your energy!* She bit her lower lip and the tears stopped. She breathed heavily.

Suddenly, her prison was moving—it felt like it was hovering through the air! She heard metal scraping against metal and screamed out. Then the cage—it had to be the trunk of a car—hit the floor with a muffled bang. The screeching metallic sounds were coming closer. What kind of metallic monster caused those sounds that drummed in her head?

She recalled the conversation she'd had with one of her clients at a networking mixer the other night. She remembered the colorful cocktail she had sipped. Everything that had followed was unknown.

.   .   .

Every time he looked at her, he appreciated why women were called *the weaker sex*. Oh, yes, they wanted to be like men and enjoy the same privileges, but they were not made to endure the same suffering. This was a sin in itself. He furiously opened the Bible and began to read in a low voice: *"A woman should learn in quietness and full submission. I do not permit a woman to teach or to assume authority over a man; she must be quiet. For Adam was formed first, then Eve. And Adam was not the one deceived; it was the woman who was deceived and became a sinner. But women will be saved through childbearing—if they continue in faith, love, and holiness with propriety."*

Those lines were from the first epistle to Timothy. He slammed the Bible shut. She was causing him far more trouble than any of the men had. He'd even had to clean up her nauseating vomit before the smell grew unbearable. He stood up and hammered against the wall so vigorously his skin opened and began to bleed. The blood left red stains on the white wallpaper. *She will pay for this, wretched sinner.* He switched off the monitors and left his control room in a furious rage.

.   .   .

Searching for DNA traces, the Forensics Department had turned Markus Heilkamp's apartment upside down. In the bathroom and kitchen of the small farmhouse just outside the Zons city limits, they secured a good amount of possibly useful material. Wrapped in plastic bags, the DNA samples sat in the corridor, waiting to be taken to the lab. On the pillows in the bedroom, the men had also found some strands of hair, which they had meticulously picked up with tweezers. In their snow-white coveralls and hoods, the guys from Forensics looked like extraterrestrials from Mars. Their disproportionately large plastic overshoes rustled as they moved through the rooms.

Oliver was wearing the Forensics garb, too, and he hated it. It reminded him of the sterile operating rooms in hospitals, and they, in turn, reminded him of his father's death. He looked around the house. They hadn't found anything that would indicate a violent crime. However, there wasn't a single suitcase in the entire house, and some clothes seemed to be missing from hangers in the closets. He wasn't sure, but everything appeared as if Markus Heilkamp had left on a trip.

Oliver glanced out the window onto a large barley field, where the ears were gently swaying in the breeze. A few large old willow trees lined the field. They cast a nice shadow, and Oliver thought it might be an ideal spot for a picnic. How he longed to live in a place like this. He wondered whether Emily would like it here and was astonished that he could picture himself with her at his side. Never before had he experienced such strong feelings for a woman. He saw them resting together beneath one of those large willow trees, enjoying a bottle of red wine. The thought made him smile.

"Well, you sure have pleasant daydreams," Klaus said, jolting Oliver out of his sweet fantasies. Then Oliver's phone rang. It was his mother again. Bad timing, as usual.

"Hi, Mom, how are you?"

"The window has been repaired, but the police said they won't investigate further. Can you believe it? They called it insignificant. How can a vandalized basement window be insignificant? Maybe someone wanted to kill me."

"Mom, please, relax. I'll have a word with them later, so you can feel entirely safe."

"Are you coming home for the weekend, sweetheart?"

Oliver scratched his head. He had other plans. He wanted to spend the weekend with Emily. He hesitated.

"What's the matter, Oliver? Don't you want to visit your mom?"

"No—I mean, yes." Oliver blushed. He quickly thought of an explanation that wouldn't hurt his mother's feelings. "We have a workshop at the academy this weekend. I'm afraid we'll have to get together another time."

He could hear the disappointment in her voice. She didn't believe him. "Well, OK, then. But promise you'll visit next weekend. I need to convince myself that you're all right."

You don't want to be alone, is what it is, Oliver thought, but he bit his tongue. He understood that she was lonely. Since his father's death, Oliver was all she had. He felt bad, but he needed to live his own life. And right now, his life pretty much consisted of Emily.

His phone rang again. This time, it was the precinct in Neuss.

"Good afternoon, Detective Bergmann. We have a young man here at the precinct who claims he found bone fragments at a parking lot on Edisonstraße, just off Highway B9, in the vicinity of Saint Peter. Thought you'd like to know immediately."

.   .   .

Emily and Anna stood in front of the county archive in the center of Zons. The tourist information center was right across the street, in a tiny medieval house. A group of visitors gathered outside, eagerly waiting for their tour to begin.

When the two friends entered the country archive, they almost bumped into Dietrich Hellenbruch. The archivist was scurrying back and forth, stuffing personal items into a bag. Despite his one limping leg, he moved about surprisingly well. He grabbed his car key and tried to rush past Emily and Anna, pretending he hadn't noticed them.

"Excuse us, we need your help!"

Hellenbruch stopped and glowered at them. Damn it, he had to get to McDonald's! Lovely Marie's shift began in fifteen minutes, and today he wanted to be the first in line. He had no time for this nuisance. The petite Italian he remembered from last winter. He still thought she was attractive—although, of course, no match for Marie. Should he just leave and ask them to return in two hours? No, his boss would not like that at all. He sighed and dropped his bag on the counter.

"I don't have much time, ladies. I remember you quite well. I've told you everything I know about the fatal-puzzle killings." He looked sternly at Emily, who immediately took a step back. He'd never look at his beloved Marie that way. Hellenbruch pushed his thick horn-rimmed glasses up his nose and smirked.

"This time," she said, "we need information about the crimes Bastian Mühlenberg investigated *after* those murders were solved. I understand that in the summer of 1496 another serial killer terrorized Zons."

"Ah, you're referring to the so-called reaping season? The lunatic who finished off sinners with his sickle? Those were particularly dark days. Everybody lived in fear of the mad Reaper. Men and women alike, he didn't care. He only spared the children, because in his eyes they were innocent. But why don't you read about it yourself? As I said, I don't have much time." He glanced at his watch. "An urgent appointment. I really must run."

With these words, he turned and hurried to the back room of the archive. Emily remembered that room well. It was much larger than one would expect and was filled with rows of dusty racks. She felt slightly uneasy when she recalled being inside that room, alone with the weird archivist, during her previous research. She was glad to have Anna's company now.

They followed the limping archivist. The room was just as dusty as Emily remembered. The rows of racks seemed endless, and it was impossible to see to the far end of the room. Hellenbruch stopped in front of a smaller rack filled with boxes of index cards. He scratched his head, thinking. Then he nodded and pulled a card box from one of the upper shelves.

"Here you go, ladies. In this box you'll find all noteworthy incidents that occurred in Zons in 1496. The records begin in May of that year. On each card there's a summary of the documents we have here and an index as to where they are. Mostly it's copies, of course. Each row of racks is marked with a capital letter. The sections are marked with Roman numerals. Sometimes you'll also see the shelf number, which spares you having to search from top to bottom. You have an hour to look for everything you need. But don't touch anything else, you hear me? I have to run now. Don't make me regret trusting you!"

He waited until he saw both Anna and Emily nod, and he limped away as fast as he could. The door slammed shut. Anna jumped. The room was cool, and the weak fluorescent lights on the ceiling flickered.

"It's eerie here," whispered Anna without taking her eyes off the racks. "I wonder how many documents they have. Thousands, certainly." Her voice was filled with admiration.

Emily, already used to the spooky atmosphere, was leafing through the index cards. Then she paused and pulled one out. "Look, Anna, Bastian Mühlenberg also kept a diary about these killings. I need to have that. It's in row B-XX."

She took a step back and studied the letters on the rows. Something was off. The first row was clearly marked with an *A*, and then came *C*, then *D, E, F* . . . But where was *B*?

"Anna, do you see row B? I can't find it."

Emily turned around, and her heart skipped.

"Anna?"

She walked past three rows and called again, louder this time.

"Anna, where are you?"

Still no answer. She felt panic creeping up inside her. Hastily, she turned around and ran back to the spot where she had last seen Anna. She could see her footprints on the dust-covered floor. They went to the left and disappeared between rows A and C.

"Found it!"

Emily saw brown curls peeking out between the two racks and let out a sigh of relief.

"You scared me, Anna," she said and ran toward her friend. It turned out that row B basically continued row A. No wonder she had been confused.

"I found the diary!"

Anna proudly lifted the diary and showed it to Emily. Then she turned her attention back to a box filled with documents and unearthed a small portrait. It was an old oil painting of Bastian Mühlenberg in his uniform, holding a lance. Anna smiled dreamily at the portrait.

"You're still convinced you actually met him, aren't you?"

Anna sighed. "Oh, Emily, you just can't imagine how it felt. I'm not sure what to make of it."

Emily took the small painting out of Anna's hands and looked at it. "Whatever it was, here's one thing for the record: he was cute. I'll give you that." She grinned at Anna and handed her back the frame.

"When's your assignment due?" asked Anna.

"Oh, I have all summer. They want it in three parts, like last year. I hope they'll like them just as much as the first series."

"I don't doubt they will," said Anna.

They skimmed through the diary and marked the parts that Emily wanted to photocopy. When Anna's phone rang and she saw it was Jimmy, she debated whether she should answer or not. Then she remembered how urgently Matthias Kronberg needed the loan green-lighted, and she answered the call.

"Hey there, sweetie," said Jimmy, "I got good news for you. Well, first you have to have dinner with me, then I'll give you the good news."

"Stop kidding yourself, Jimmy. I promised my client an answer by today. It's almost evening and I still haven't called him back."

"You're always so tense," said Jimmy.

"It's because I've been staring at my phone all day and still haven't heard from the risk-assessment people. Did you speak with them?"

"Not directly. But if you manage to sell him my new swap, they'll up the limit."

"Is that so?" Anna was surprised. That was news to her.

"Yep, order from the top brass. If you have dinner with me, I'll send you the minutes of the board meeting and you can light a fire under the risk people's behinds. Well, if your client buys the swap, that is."

"I already explained the deal to him." He didn't have much of a choice, anyway. Kronberg needed money, and with that money he would have to make some good investment decisions. Otherwise the jig was up. "We're still talking about the yen swaps, right?"

"Yep, honey bun, and the prospects are rosy. Trust me!"

Anna didn't need to think twice. If the deal went bad, her client would be bankrupt three weeks earlier than he'd be if he didn't do anything. Three weeks didn't make much of a difference. She would have to be very clear in explaining the situation, but at least the yen swap gave him a chance. His alternative was to declare Chapter Eleven now and tell his wife.

"Sounds good. Send me the minutes and I'll call the Risk Management Department."

"I need your promise first. Dinner for two," he said.

Anna rolled her eyes. That was so typical of Jimmy, he wouldn't give up. "I have a reception with clients this Friday. Can you make do with having a bite with me there?"

"Only if you promise to have a cocktail with me, too, pumpkin."

"OK, deal."

.   .   .

Dumbfounded, Oliver stood in the parking lot just off Highway B9, where the young man had found the new bone fragments. Klaus, standing next to Oliver, frowned.

"Why are you so sure it's another foot? Did you suddenly become an expert on foot-bone fragments?"

"No, I just use my mouth to ask questions." Oliver grinned and motioned behind him. Klaus followed the movement and saw someone from Forensics arrive with Frau Scholten, the head of the Crime Lab.

"What's she doing here?"

"Steuermark sent her. He thinks it's highly unlikely that a second bone fragment appears and there's no crime involved. To be honest, I agree with him." Oliver scratched his chin. The first finding had occurred in the Rhine meadows near Zons. Now they were standing in a parking lot that bordered a huge barley field. "Klaus, the first find was next to a barley field as well, wasn't it?"

"Yep. This area's full of barley fields. Lots of farmers around Zons. Why?"

"Maybe there's a connection."

Oliver walked along the edge that separated the crops from the parking lot. The stalks were bowing in the wind. The sky was bright, with only a few fleecy clouds here and there. It was a perfect summer day. But then the wind turned and blew over an unpleasant smell. Oliver sniffed. He recognized the nauseating odor: it was dung. This field had recently been fertilized. He tried to recall the other site and remembered that the smell had been the same. Klaus had covered his nose with a handkerchief there, because bad odors usually gave him an allergic reaction. Oliver glanced at Klaus now. He was already fishing a used handkerchief out of his pocket and covering his mouth and nose.

"What?" Klaus said. "You know full well I can't stand these smells. I'm not a hayseed like you. The idea of a country house makes me want to run away. I love my apartment in the city and the smell of gasoline."

"Yeah, I know. But don't you remember the barley field that was next to the first find? That field had also just been fertilized."

"So what? The farmers follow their calendar. That explains why it literally stinks everywhere around here!"

Oliver shook his head. His gut feeling told him the two findings were connected. But first he needed to prove something. He reached for his phone and called Steuermark.

"I need approval for a canine unit. Three dogs will do."

.   .   .

Soon after the phone call, three large unmarked cars with their hidden blue lights switched on drove into the parking lot and stopped in front of Oliver and Klaus with screeching tires. The doors on the sides of the vehicles slid open, and athletic, muscular men in dark-blue uniforms and black boots jumped out. The loud barking of dogs accompanied the dramatic performance. The policemen opened the transport boxes, and three German shepherds jumped out, wagging their tails. One of the men blew a whistle, and the dogs were instantly silent.

"Are you Bergmann?"

Oliver nodded. He was impressed.

"Where did he find the bone fragments?"

Oliver pointed over to the site at the border of the parking lot. Forensics had marked the spot with a little red flag. The leader of the dog squad gathered his men to discuss the situation. They divided the field into several quadrants that they would systematically comb. Before they began, the dogs sniffed at the bone.

Only fifty yards away from where the bone had been found, a huge dog named Alex gave the first bark. His dark fur shone in the sunlight, and he panted with excitement. His master recognized the signal the dog gave him—and, indeed, Alex had found another bone fragment. Soon after that, another dog found more fragments at the far edge of the field. After only half an hour, the dogs had found six more pieces.

"It's likely there are even more human bone fragments, but what with the aggressive odor from the manure, my dogs can't perform one hundred percent. We can return in a few days."

Oliver nodded, wondering why the bones had been dispersed across the field. Why had the killer not buried them? It would have been so much easier. Oliver looked at the seven little red flags. He couldn't recognize a pattern. From whatever angle he regarded the constellation of flags, it seemed arbitrary and chaotic. Something seemed off. Why just scatter the bones? What kind of method had the killer or killers used? Had they even used one at all?

An angry voice roused him out of his thoughts. "What are you doing here with your wild beasts trampling my field? Get off my property!"

A chubby-cheeked man came stomping toward them. He was in his sixties and had on rubber boots, dark corduroy pants, and a baggy checkered shirt. He tried to break into the cordoned-off area. Alex growled, but that didn't hold the furious farmer back.

"Good afternoon," Oliver said to him. "We're conducting a police investigation. What's your name?"

"Fritz Kallenbach, and I don't allow anyone to walk on my field and ruin my crops."

The farmer's face grew increasingly red, and Oliver began to worry. Fritz Kallenbach straightened himself to his full height—and considerable width—and glowered at the two detectives.

"Herr Kallenbach. We're very sorry that we couldn't give you a heads-up, but we're investigating what might be a capital crime. We've discovered several fragments of a human body on your field. Could you tell us how they got here?"

"What do you mean, fragments of a human body?"

Suddenly, Kallenbach's attention was captured by the box that held the plastic bags with the bones. All the color drained from his face. He took a few steps back.

"That's impossible!"

"We need to know, what was the last thing done on this field, and who worked here that day?"

"I do this all myself. But it wasn't me!"

Kallenbach's stout body seemed suddenly weak; he began to sway back and forth. Klaus jumped to his side and tried to support the staggering man, who was in a state of shock.

"Let's sit down first. Once you've calmed down, we'll have all the time in the world for you to tell us what kind of work you've been doing here over the past couple of weeks."

While he was speaking, Klaus slowly led the farmer over to one of the vans and offered him a seat inside. Still swaying and breathing heavily, Kallenbach pulled a crumpled handkerchief out of his pocket. He slowly dabbed the sweat from his forehead. Klaus waited until the man was done before he asked in a soothing voice, "When were you last here on your field, Herr Kallenbach?"

"With the boy, a week ago. I showed him exactly how to go about the fertilizing."

"So you don't work entirely by yourself?"

"No, Frederick takes care of this. He's making some money on the side. Poor kid. He's not the brightest, if you know what I mean, but he does know how to drive the tractor and spread manure." The old farmer coughed, and his face turned deep red again.

"Frederick is my cousin's son. He came far too early into this world, and for a while it looked as if he wouldn't stay long, but he made it, the little preemie. Everyone had given up on him. Well, the good Lord gave him his life and a healthy body, but not too much in the brains. They call him mentally challenged."

"Besides the two of you, no one else was on the field?"

"No, I already told you that!"

"Did you notice anything out of the norm? Maybe suspiciously parked vehicles or strangers loitering around your field?"

"No, I've got everything under control. I immediately noticed you, didn't I!"

.　.　.

"Good morning, Jimmy. You seem bored at work!" Anna was standing behind Jimmy; he was looking at his Facebook page. Among his many contacts, Anna recognized some familiar faces from the bank.

"What are you doing here so early?" Jimmy quickly closed the page and turned around. His cheeks were burning red.

"I wanted to thank you, that's all. Risk Management has given the OK for the loan. Now my client has a chance to save his company from bankruptcy."

"Aw, and you came in early to tell me that, my dear? You're not going to cancel on me for Friday night, are you?"

"No, Jimmy. I just wanted to thank you in person. Without the board's intervention, it would have taken too long, and I might still be waiting to get an answer from the Risk Management Department."

Anna's phone rang. She quickly pulled it out of her pocket and checked the display. Matthias Kronberg. He must have finally listened to her voice mail. She had tried several times to reach him yesterday evening. She exchanged a glance with Jimmy, shrugged, and answered. "Good morning, Herr Kronberg. I hope you got the good news? I couldn't reach you yesterday."

"Thank you, Frau Winterfeld. I had an important appointment yesterday and no signal."

A loud, shrill whistling sound cut them off for a moment. Anna held the phone away from her ear. The jarring noise was so loud that Jimmy heard it, too.

"Hello? Hello, Herr Kronberg, are you still there?"

The noise stopped for a few seconds, and Anna could dimly hear her client's voice. Then the line went dead.

Jimmy was staring intently at his Facebook page again. Anna tried to catch a glimpse of the open profile, but Jimmy sensed she was looking and clicked it away. Anna saw that it was a woman's profile. She looked familiar, but Anna couldn't think of her name.

Just when she wanted to say something to Jimmy, her phone rang again. This time, it was Emily. She probably wanted to fill Anna in on her date with Oliver the night before. Anna couldn't wait to hear all about it.

"So sorry, Jimmy, but I have to run. I'll see you on Friday!"

.   .   .

Oliver frowned as he leafed through the pages of the lab reports. Then he studied the profiles of the five missing persons again. By now the canine unit had completed searching Kallenbach's field as well as parts of the bordering Rhine meadows. Their search had yielded three more bone fragments. Oliver suspected that a stray dog had carried the first bone—the one the couple had found during their picnic—to the Rhine meadows and buried it there.

The lab was in full swing. Police had already dismissed the two Russian men as potential victims. While Oliver thought the Russian Mafia was very capable of making bodies disappear with the aid of hydrochloric acid, the results had been convincingly clear. His previously most promising lead had also proved insubstantial. The DNA of the missing chemist and manager of the hydrochloric-acid tanks, forty-nine-year-old Markus Heilkamp, did not match the DNA of the bone fragments.

There remained only two possible victims: Peter Schreiner, a man of forty-six who worked as a mechanic at a garage in Dormagen, and Peter Hirschauer, the forty-nine-year-old banker who had recently been laid off and whose disappearance continued to be a mystery.

The police suspected that Peter Schreiner had left his wife and was keeping a low profile. Oliver thought for a moment. He and Klaus had agreed to wait for the new lab reports before they would take any action, but an inner voice kept telling Oliver he should focus on Peter Hirschauer. It wouldn't hurt to search the banker's house for DNA. He'd suggest it to his boss. Steuermark liked for things to move quickly, and Oliver was positive he'd get a search warrant, despite the lack of substantial evidence. He glanced at his watch. Where the heck was Klaus? They still needed to get after Frederick Köppe, the man who worked for Kallenbach.

Oliver's phone rang.

"We have a female body, in a car wash on Highway B9, in Zons. Come right away!"

.   .   .

He had hardly slept all night. What a mistake! They had almost seen him. The thought of it made him shudder. On his computer, he thoroughly scanned the images from the various surveillance cameras. Everything seemed quiet. Then he began checking his regular websites.

He spent some time on Facebook and LinkedIn. Three of his targets had public profiles. He clicked on the photo of a pretty brunette. When he zoomed in, her emerald eyes smiled at him. *Here's another sinner,* he thought and felt cold wrath welling up inside him. He wondered if she was as weak as the one before her, the one he had sent through purgatory with God's help. Then he clicked on another profile. Another candidate who had committed a deadly sin looked at him. Money never slept. Nor did God!

He put one hand on the Bible, closed his eyes, and said a prayer. It felt good, murmuring the Latin words. Then he chanted a tune that had filled God's cathedrals for centuries on end. He began to relax. Outside, in the early morning dawn, everything was quiet. If he was lucky, nobody would ever discover his secret.

He felt another shiver down his spine when he recalled the previous night. As always, he had prepared everything perfectly. The site where he executed God's judgment was deserted. Nobody ever came there at night—except for last night. Just when he was cutting through that godless sinner's throat with his golden sickle, a loud bawling and roaring had disturbed him.

He'd dropped the body and sneaked over to the small window of the car wash. He didn't usually feel fear, but he couldn't deny that he was concerned as he peeked outside. Windowpanes shattered. A group of drunken teens stumbled along the country road, chanting their idiotic drinking songs through the quiet night.

Apparently, they were after the booze in the gas station's store. But the alarm went off with a deafening noise, and he decided to split. He'd barely managed to clean up the most visible traces before the police arrived. He'd shoved the body into a hatch in the floor where they usually kept the maintenance tools. He'd had to cram the body a bit, but she was petite, so she fit. He hoped nobody would find her; he planned to return and make her disappear forever. And he had taken precautionary measures. Besides, the world was full of sinners. He could follow his calling anywhere.

.   .   .

"Look, Anna! Isn't this amazing?" Emily dangled three small, ancient keys in front of Anna's face.

"Where did you get these?"

"In the county archive. They were hidden in a dust-covered box at the end of a shelf. I went back the other day and the old weirdo let me research alone again."

Emily flipped through the photocopied pages of Bastian Mühlenberg's journal. She slid a finger along the lines and stopped in the middle of a page. She concentrated hard to decipher the handwriting, but she was too overwhelmed with excitement. Her cheeks were flushed, and she brushed stray strands of hair from her face. She already knew how her new feature series would shape up. She had the feeling that these three keys were of great significance. The investigative journalist in her picked up the scent of a suspenseful story that would reveal a forgotten secret that had been hidden for centuries.

"Weren't you going to tell me about your date with Oliver?" Anna was bored. She leaned against the radiator at the window in Emily's bedroom. The keys weren't particularly interesting to her. And Emily didn't even react to her question. She had spread the material all across her bed and on the floor and was reading intently. Then she looked up at Anna.

"These entries are confusing. Everything I've read so far from Bastian Mühlenberg was very precise and comprehensive. But here his writing gets twisted. In the previous chapters he wrote about the Fraternity of Saint Sebastian in Zons and a murdered standard-bearer named Benedict Eschenbach. What follows is a brief paragraph about some missing people. They all disappeared within a couple of months. For example, Doctor Josef Hesemann's cousin. His name was Conrad, and he was a monk at Knechtsteden Abbey. Apparently he visited Zons often and helped Josef with the sick—cared for them and gave comfort. Then the writing just ends. Bastian mentions a meeting with Father Johannes, and then he only draws symbols that look like hieroglyphs. These three could be keys. Then on the next page, he draws a large key."

Emily laid one of the keys over the drawings. The contours matched perfectly.

"Look at this, Anna!"

Anna frowned. She remembered how Emily, during her previous assignment, had deciphered most of the old handwriting in another of Bastian's diaries with astounding ease. Yet the course of time had damaged some of these pages, the many centuries having left their mark, and the photocopies were basically illegible.

"Didn't you have an expert restore the damaged pages last time?"

"Yes, but that was different. These symbols aren't blurry or smudged. Look for yourself."

Anna really would have preferred to talk with Emily about Oliver. She longed to fall in love again herself, and she really couldn't understand Emily's obsession with her assignment; it was only a job.

Anna noticed a piece of paper at her feet. It was a thin piece of parchment with ragged edges, which had been lying underneath the radiator.

"What's that old paper doing there?"

XI
Five Hundred Years Ago

Bastian put the third key on a new page in his diary and, with a thin quill, copied the key's exact contours onto the paper. Wernhart was lying in a bed next to the desk. He moaned again. The poor fellow still suffered from stomach cramps. The castor oil Josef had prescribed was even more efficient than the doctor had expected. Bastian felt sorry for Wernhart. His face was green and pale. Then again, without the castor oil they wouldn't have retrieved the key Wernhart had swallowed. Josef had made a good call in suggesting they speed up Wernhart's digestion. After all, they couldn't cut him open.

Josef entered the small room carrying a big jar of water. "Drink, Wernhart. Your body needs the liquid. We're no different from the plants, you know. We dry out without water."

Wernhart drank the cool, refreshing water. He wiped his lips, and, for a brief moment, the sickly green disappeared from his face. Exhausted, he fell back on the pillows.

"Bastian, before you go to Father Johannes, there's something I need to tell you."

Josef was about to give the two city guards their privacy, but Bastian grabbed his sleeve and held him back.

"Stay, Josef. I trust your discretion and loyalty."

The doctor nodded and took a seat next to Bastian.

His voice trembling, Wernhart began to speak. "That night, in Huppertz's house, I discovered a large container of gold coins. At least two hundred guldens."

"Are you sure?"

Wernhart nodded and held a hand over his aching stomach.

"Where would he get so much gold?"

"Maybe he robbed his own fraternity brothers and took the gold from the famous chest."

"But he needs three keys to open the chest!"

Josef nodded and said, "What if he took the money a long time ago?"

Bastian glanced at Josef in surprise, then slapped his hand on his thigh. "Absolutely! He stole it, and Benedict Eschenbach saw the coins. Maybe he tried to get a hold of all three keys, so he could open the chest and confirm his suspicion. Huppertz wanted to prevent that, obviously, and had Eschenbach killed as soon as he had the first key in his hands."

Wernhart raised himself, terrified. "You're saying Huppertz murdered Benedict?"

"It's possible."

Bastian scribbled notes in his diary. He had to make sure he would remember these thoughts. So far, he hadn't discovered the slightest trace that might lead him to the person who'd killed Benedict. Quite annoying for him, especially because old Jacob had basically witnessed the crime yet remembered nothing but a fleeting shadow. There was always a motive for murder, and Bastian knew he had found it. Suddenly he understood why Huppertz had not reported Wernhart's trespassing to the City Guard, as one would have assumed he would. Now he saw it clearly. Huppertz didn't want anybody to investigate and stumble over the gold coins in his house, because he didn't want to answer any questions. Bastian let out a sigh. It was a miracle the man hadn't killed Wernhart.

"You were very lucky," Bastian said to Wernhart.

Wernhart nodded. "I know. Had I not discovered the gold, I'd be either in the dungeon or dead."

The door swung open and Margarete, Josef's wife, ran toward Josef. Her eyes were red, and she was sobbing. "Conrad has disappeared. I just spoke with the abbot. Ludwig von Monheim says he hasn't seen Conrad for several days. Oh, dear Lord, have mercy! Something terrible must have happened to him!"

She buried her face in her hands and tried to hide her tears. Josef hugged her and looked at Bastian for support. Bastian rose from his seat and walked over to Margarete.

"I assure you that the City Guard will be looking for Conrad as soon as possible. I'm sure nothing happened and that he'll resurface safe and sound."

"But old Jacob's wife has been missing for three days as well," Margarete sobbed. "Don't you find this strange? One might suspect Dietrich Hellenbroich has returned to torture us again."

Upon hearing the name of the notorious serial killer from the year before, Bastian cringed. That wasn't possible. The fatal puzzle was solved. And even if it wasn't, Hellenbroich was only interested in young girls.

"Listen, Margarete," said Bastian, "old Jacob hasn't even come to inform me yet that his wife is missing. She sometimes sneaks off to her daughter's. I bet you're well aware that their marriage is not the best. If Jacob believed something was off, he'd come and see me, don't you think?"

Margarete's sobbing grew louder as she gave Bastian an annoyed look. "He said he was only going to wait until tonight. Trust me, Bastian, something is wrong!"

"I'll look into it when he contacts me tomorrow, I give you my word."

. . .

Huppertz was beside himself. That moron Wilhelm was completely useless. Not only had he failed in watching Wernhart in his cell for a few hours, but he also had somehow let himself be gagged and tied to a chair at Huppertz's kitchen table, and now he was weeping like a little girl—or trying to, through the gag.

"What happened while I was away?" thundered Huppertz. His voice almost cracked, and Wilhelm stared at him in fear. Huppertz tore the gag out of his mouth. "Did Wernhart do that?"

"No, it was the Devil," Wilhelm said, whining.

Huppertz had really had enough of this baby. "Couldn't you just handle this one simple task? Where's Katharina?"

"He took her with him." Tears were streaming down Wilhelm's face.

"What do you mean?" Huppertz was about to explode and violently shook the helpless man. Then he took off his fetters. Wilhelm rubbed his arms. His skin was bruised. He had tried to free himself.

"First he chained the three of us, but then he decided to let Wernhart run." Wilhelm shook his head and cried some more. His voice was barely audible when he said, "In the end, he grabbed Katharina and dragged her away. I couldn't do anything, really! I'm so sorry!"

Wilhelm's long, high-pitched wailing reminded Huppertz of a dog's howling. Looking at this miserable loser, Huppertz could barely restrain himself. He really wanted to beat him. Damn it, this idiot was supposed to stand guard. Now Wernhart had escaped and, even worse, Katharina was gone.

In a rage, Huppertz took his sharpest sword out of the closet. He would go to the City Guard right now and complain. He'd had it! That Wernhart should give him back Katharina. If he didn't get her back, he was ready for anything. He didn't have the patience for long negotiations. They'd either give him Katharina, or he'd slaughter every man from the City Guard. His face crimson, he dashed out of the house and hurried toward Bastian's place next to the Mühlenturm.

Midway, Huppertz stopped. One of Wilhelm's sentences had struck him: *It was the Devil.*

What if Bastian Mühlenberg had no idea what Wernhart was doing? Or if Wilhelm was right, and Katharina had been kidnapped not by Wernhart but by some unknown evildoer, then Huppertz was on the wrong track altogether. He had to return and talk with Wilhelm again. That idiot needed to describe in painstaking detail the devil he had seen.

·　·　·

His thick, calloused fingers caressed a page of the Bible. He had read this passage so many times that his frequent touch had caused the print to become blurry and smudged. In other parts, some letters had faded so much the text was illegible. But he didn't mind. He knew the passage by heart, anyway. A familiar tune began to fill his head again. It had been a faithful companion since his childhood. *Art Thou angry, my Lord?* He wasn't sure whether he had done the right thing. He reached under the table and pulled out a whip. It was a cat-o'-nine-tails, each "tail" fastened with tiny metallic spikes. He hummed the tune out loud and whipped the skin on his back as hard as he could. The whip hissed through the air.

But it didn't hurt more than it usually did. So he had done everything right. Yet because he wasn't entirely sure whether he had interpreted God's answer correctly, he raised his arm high and whipped his back again. Only now could he be certain that the pain had not intensified. This reassured him. He sighed and put the whip back under the table. He resumed reading. Outside, a church bell tolled. He got up and looked out the window. It was time.

His secret place was best reached in broad daylight—the place where he carried out God's mission. The place where he taught sinners that God did not approve of lies and letters of indulgence. It was a deadly sin, to think that one could buy his way out of hell. Only evil fools would think they could buy God's mercy.

He vividly remembered the day, many years ago, when that indulgence preacher Tetzel had visited. Since then, their paths hadn't crossed again, thank God. Yet he still recalled the haughty preacher as if it had been yesterday—how he had reveled in the excessive complacency of his speech. Nothing but pure blasphemy. But the abbot, Ludwig von Monheim, was riveted. He would never forget the pain that cut through his heart when he saw the abbot pat Tetzel's shoulder and congratulate him. How he had blushed when he saw all the guldens Tetzel had gained after only one day of selling indulgence letters. Granted, Knechtsteden Abbey surely profited from the money, but there would have been a more blessed way to secure its survival.

His thoughts turned to the previous night. The two women weren't half as bad as that son of a bitch Johann Tetzel. But still, they had sinned and needed punishment. It was acceptable that he had enjoyed the chastening of those two sinners in one go.

Are you sure? a doubtful voice asked inside him.

He didn't want to listen to that voice. If he had done something wrong, God would have punished him with pain. But that hadn't happened.

But you did enjoy seeing those two tarts suffer, didn't you? The voice would not stop.

Of course he'd enjoyed it. What was wrong with finding pleasure in carrying out God's work?

But that wasn't the only way in which you enjoyed it. The voice wanted to drive him over the edge.

No, he had not wanted it. At least, he had not intended it. Yet the growing arousal he felt between his thighs reminded him all too clearly of the lust that had taken control of him when he'd whipped the first woman's bare breasts. Her tortured moaning excited him even more, and then her beautiful breasts were destroyed. He regretted it only briefly. He wasn't at fault here. Anxiously, he flipped back to another of his favorite passages, the lines in the first epistle to Timothy: *Adam was not the one deceived; it was the woman who was deceived and became a sinner.*

They were fully responsible for what had happened to them. He furiously slammed shut the Holy Scripture. Soon, the bell would toll again. He had to leave; it was time for the next sinner to go to hell!

.　　.　　.

The smell of fresh frankincense wafted through the church. Bastian inhaled deeply and enjoyed the familiar aroma. It evoked pleasant images from his childhood. He recalled the many lessons with Father Johannes, when the priest taught him how to read and write. He remembered the letters made out of wood that he used to form new words at the clergyman's request. Bastian had enjoyed the game and taken a particular pleasure in arranging the letters into new words faster and faster. He could still feel the pride that had filled him when he had first been allowed to use ink, quill, and real paper.

His heart had beat fast because he dreaded that he might make a mess on the precious paper.

The feel of thick, calloused fingers on his shoulder jolted him out of his memories, and Bastian jumped and turned around. It was Brother Ignatius.

"I've spoken to your brother Albrecht. Tasks at the monastery keep him very busy, but he promised to visit Heinrich at his sickbed this week. Also, I've just visited Heinrich myself. He seems to be doing much better."

"Really? Such wonderful news," said Bastian, elated. He had a guilty conscience for not having visited Heinrich recently, but now he felt relief. He knew it: his big brother was indestructible. He had worried for nothing. Heinrich was recovering, and that meant Bastian wouldn't need to fulfill his brother's last wish anytime soon.

Suddenly, Father Johannes came rushing toward him in his rustling, precious habit adorned with golden embroidery. He hadn't changed after mass. He hugged Bastian and kissed his cheek. "Follow me into the vestibule, my dear boy," he whispered.

Bastian obeyed. He nodded at Brother Ignatius, who, in his modest, dark-brown monk's cloak, looked rather plain compared to Father Johannes. Then Bastian followed the priest, who was walking so fast Bastian almost couldn't keep up. Johannes closed the door to the vestibule and said, "Oh, Bastian. I can see it in your face! You found the third key, am I right?"

"You're astute, Father Johannes!"

Bastian smiled when he pulled out the key and handed it over.

"You really did it. I'm so proud of you, my boy."

Father Johannes held up the key in awe and turned it back and forth between his fingers. Then he put it on the table and, with Bastian's help, pushed the heavy oak armoire to the side. Again it scratched over the church's stone flooring. Like the previous time, the priest felt along the wall until he reached the tiny lever, and the wall opened up a crack. Johannes put the linen cloth on the table and opened it. He arranged the three keys in a neat line and beheld them in stunned admiration.

"Imagine, Bastian, these keys haven't been reunited for more than a hundred years."

Bastian frowned. He remembered what Josef had suggested that morning. "Father Johannes, I don't want to upset you, but it's possible the chest has already been opened."

The old priest stared at Bastian in disbelief. His face was pale. He put a hand on his chest and breathed heavily. "Bastian, it's not funny to scare an old man! What do you mean, the chest has already been opened?"

"Wernhart stole the key from Huppertz's house. He told me there are at least two hundred gold coins inside the house. Huppertz caught Wernhart but did not report him to the City Guard. If his conscience were clean, he'd have had Wernhart interrogated immediately."

"You stole the key from his house?"

Ashamed, Bastian lowered his head. "Father Johannes, there was no other way. How else would I have been able to bring you the third key?"

The priest crossed himself. "Well, dear boy, we shall revisit this later. First we need to determine whether the chest has indeed been opened. Let's hope and pray that the archbishop's legacy has not vanished!"

Father Johannes wrapped the old linen cloth around the keys and hid the small bundle under his habit. Then he asked Bastian to push the heavy oak armoire back to its place. He opened the door of the vestibule and peeked outside. Brother Ignatius was nowhere to be seen. Johannes was relieved and opened the door wide. He and Bastian stepped into the hallway.

"Where's Ignatius?"

"He was very pressed for time after mass. Many responsibilities wait for him at the monastery. In fact, I'm glad he's not here anymore, because he's not supposed to see what I will show you in just one moment. Come with me!"

The priest pattered through the nave of the church and climbed down the steps to the crypt. Cold, musty air greeted them when he opened the heavy door that led to the vault. Bastian began to shiver. He didn't like this place. As a boy, he'd always been frightened down here. It was not only dark and cold, but also damp. Thousands of tiny water drops were trickling down from the vaulted ceiling and along the rough stone walls. Their rhythmic echo bounced against the walls.

Johannes paused to grab a large candle. He kindled it with the flame of a smaller candle that was always burning down here in order to provide some light and orientation.

"That way!" He beckoned Bastian to follow him. "It's here. We're directly underneath the Saint Sebastianus altar. Do you see the bow? That is the bow Numidian archers used to attack the holy Sebastian. This arrow here pierced through Sebastian's flesh."

Bastian was stunned. He was in awe as he touched the heavy old wooden bow. The wood felt brittle. Then he turned his attention back to Father Johannes, who was pushing aside a heavy stone plate on the floor. Both men looked into an abyss. Johannes held up the candle, and Bastian could make out rough-hewn steps leading into the darkness. Father Johannes walked down the stairs. Bastian followed, feeling queasy. The steps were slippery. Carefully, the men continued down the seemingly endless stairs. The candle flame flickered around Father Johannes's head and illuminated the vaulted ceiling. The ceiling was so low that Bastian had to duck. Father Johannes, who was much shorter, could easily stand erect.

They arrived in a tiny room. The walls, illuminated by the candle, appeared to be made of sharp-edged rocks—the same material that had been used to build the stairs and vault. Cockroaches scurried to the nearest dark cracks. Finally, the light fell onto a large, beautifully ornamented chest.

"Here it is!"

There were three locks on the chest. Father Johannes pulled out the linen bundle from underneath his habit and removed the three keys, which he carefully inserted into their respective locks. But then he hesitated and scratched his head.

"Well, the keys must be turned in a specific order. If we start with the wrong key, the little acid vials will open and destroy the contents. I'm not sure if I remember the right order!"

He looked to be in despair, but then a memory flashed through him, and he smiled. Truly, he was getting older. How could he have forgotten this detail? He grabbed the candle and walked back to the stairs. After he had taken three steps, he paused and turned around.

"Bastian, I'm too short and my eyesight is poor. Please come and help me."

Bastian took the candle and held it against the rocky wall. At first he didn't see anything, but then he recognized a small drawing carved into the stones. The contours of the symbols had faded and were hard to discern, but after he had stared at it for a while, Bastian understood the correct order. The key on the left side had to be turned first, followed by the key on the right, and then the key in the front.

"Left, right, front," Bastian whispered, and Father Johannes hurried back into the dark vault. Bastian followed. Their hearts were beating furiously as they opened the chest—and froze in shock. Nothing! Emptiness. Bastian's heart skipped. He had been right. Huppertz had plundered the treasure.

Father Johannes wasn't shocked at all. With apt fingers he felt along the edge of the chest until he suddenly pulled out a black cloth. It was an illusion, a false bottom giving the chest the appearance of being empty. But their feelings of relief didn't last long. Father Johannes let out a startled scream.

"The gold is gone!"

He crossed himself. Then he pulled out another black cloth and opened the wooden bottom of the chest hiding underneath.

"Thank the Lord. He didn't find the map. The secret is still safe."

Now Johannes sighed with relief, holding one hand over his heart. Clearly the excitement was wearing him out. He took a deep breath and reached again into the chest. He produced an old, yellowed parchment scroll that was closed with a thick, red wax seal. Satisfied, the priest sat down on an edge of the chest and handed the scroll to Bastian.

"What is it?"

"The map of the maze."

"What maze, Father Johannes?"

"Underneath our city lies an intricate labyrinth. When Archbishop von Saarwerden granted Zons the privilege to levy customs tolls, it wasn't for the city's favorable location on the Rhine. Saarwerden wanted control over the maze."

"There's an underground maze in Zons?" Bastian was dumbfounded.

"Yes. Back in Archbishop von Saarwerden's time, everybody knew about it, but the archbishop did his best to make people forget."

"Why? And why was he so obsessed with the labyrinth? Doesn't our city's wealth stem from the formidable customs tolls we levy?"

"My dear, smart Bastian. Sometimes it's not the money alone that brings us salvation. The archbishop needed to hide a secret, a secret so important it couldn't be measured in gold!"

"What kind of secret? Please, tell me!"

The young man's impatience made the old priest laugh.

"Let's go back up, Bastian. In the light of day it will be easier to explain the map to you and make you understand what is hiding beneath our city."

Father Johannes rose and walked up the stone stairs. He was visibly exhausted, panting and moaning with each step. Bastian followed, but his thoughts were in chaos. An underground maze beneath his everyday streets! He could hardly believe it, and he fought off the urge to carry Father Johannes up the stairs like a flour sack, just to speed things up. His nagging impatience was driving him crazy.

Finally, they were back in the church and walked to the small vestibule behind the altar. Johannes slumped into a chair.

"May I open the seal and look at the map?"

"Go ahead, my friend. I like when you satisfy your quest for knowledge. Be sure to memorize its layout, because you'll have to go and fetch something for me."

"The archbishop's secret?"

The priest nodded and wiped the sweat from his forehead with a cloth. Bastian contemplated the thick, red wax seal that belonged to the Archbishop of Cologne. He identified the archbishop as the person sitting in the middle of the seal. To his left was the coat of arms of the city of Saarwerden, with its double-headed eagle. To the right, Bastian recognized the coat of arms of the archdiocese of Cologne, with its large cross. Reverentially, Bastian opened the seal and unfolded the parchment. The map depicted numerous winding paths. At its southern end, the maze reached well beyond the city's fortification. As the head of the City Guard, Bastian was shocked. He was looking at a secret loophole that could help anybody circumvent the city's gates.

"Don't you worry, Bastian. Nobody knows this secret portal exists. Even I didn't know about it until now."

"How can you be so sure?"

"Zons is invulnerable to invasion. The archbishop would never have allowed the tiniest access point. Leading experts built the fortification, and in more than a hundred years, nobody has ever managed to take the city. My confidence in our walls is solid as a rock."

Bastian frowned and decided to bring this up again later. Right now, he was more interested in the treasure that Saarwerden had hid underneath his hometown. He let his fingers run along the countless lines of the labyrinth. Several hundred paths, crisscrossing underneath the familiar squares and alleys. South of the tower that served as a prison, the so-called *Juddeturm*, he spotted a tiny image of the double-headed eagle. He pointed at it. That had to be the place!

"Is that where the treasure's hidden, Father Johannes?"

"What an intelligent lad you are, Bastian. I assume you're right. But I have to admit that the exact spot was not revealed to me. The only thing I knew was that this map exists, and that I am commanded to ensure the treasure's safety as soon as two of the three keys appear in the same place, at the same time. There are three designated bearers of the keys, two members of the Fraternity of Saint Sebastian and . . ." The priest paused and looked quizzically at Bastian, who had begun to copy Father Johannes's words into his notebook. With a quick motion of the hand, the priest ordered him to stop. "Bastian, I'm confiding a secret that has been passed on orally from generation to generation. Nobody has ever written it down. So what are you doing? Do you want to risk writing down the secret and have it fall into the wrong hands?"

"You're right. I apologize."

Bastian shut the notebook. He would have to memorize everything. Maybe he could manage to come up with some encrypted sketches that would serve as hints for himself.

"Well, so there are three designated bearers of the keys: two members of the fraternity, and one key is always with the priest. It is now upon me to transfer the treasure to its new place. I will be the only one to know where that is, and I shall reveal the location to my successor only when my last days are near. But since I trust you—and since I'm clearly in no condition to crawl underground, what with my damaged legs and aching back—I ask you to help me. Besides, there is no suitable successor anywhere on the horizon."

"Will you tell me what kind of treasure it is?"

"I'm unsure whether I should burden you with this knowledge, my dear friend. Some secrets drag heavily on our souls, and sometimes it is difficult to carry the weight of knowledge that must not be put to use."

Bastian almost burst with curiosity. Why did Father Johannes torture him so? Hadn't he proven that he could handle any secret?

The old man cast a long, searching look at Bastian and sighed. "All right, then, I shall let you in on the secret. What the archbishop hid was a blessed powder, a unique remedy that cures the plague and other terminal illnesses. Because the city walls form a narrow circle around Zons, rendering the city basically doomed in the event of an outbreak of plague, he hid a remedy inside the labyrinth in order to rescue the city in an emergency. That remedy, a powder, is stashed inside a valuable golden statue of the Holy Mary, adorned with precious jewels. Whoever gains possession of this treasure would be incredibly rich—for the statue's worth alone, but also because he'd have in his hands the cure for any illness that might befall him. That's why you need to bring the Holy Mary to her new secret place for me as fast as you can, Bastian."

Smiling, the priest patted Bastian's shoulder. The young city guard frowned. An urgent question came to mind.

"Does the powder heal lung diseases as well?"

Terrified, Johannes looked at Bastian and scolded him by wagging a finger.

"Bastian, I warned you about the burden of knowledge. According to the archbishop's will, the powder is solely for the protection of the city. It is not meant to cure individual loved ones. Do not abuse this knowledge—no matter how much you care for someone."

.   .   .

Bastian was furious. How could Marie be so careless?

"Bastian, it's only Wilhelm! Calm down already!"

Bastian peeked through the crack of the open door and saw Wilhelm at their kitchen table. Wilhelm's eyes were red and his flushed face was swollen. With his head buried in his hands, he looked pitiful. Still, Bastian was enraged. How could Marie open their house to another man? She had been alone—and even if it didn't seem particularly dangerous, it simply wasn't an appropriate thing for a married woman to do. Knowing full well he had no reason to, Bastian felt a burning jealousy that destroyed every rational thought. Marie was his. He was the only man allowed to dwell with her under this roof.

Then he took a deep breath.

He looked at Marie. Her cheeks were reddened with excitement, and her eyes sparkled with defiance.

"Marie, I'm trying to understand you. What does this poor simpleton want from us?"

"Katharina, Huppertz Helpenstein's wife, was kidnapped by the Devil!"

She spoke the last words with such conviction that Bastian couldn't help but snort with laughter.

"The Devil? Marie, you know full well that Wilhelm has always been a baby. One thing I can assure you, it was not the Devil. What would the Devil want with Katharina Helpenstein?"

The defiance and anger in Marie's eyes intensified. "You just refuse to see it, don't you? Now Katharina is missing, too. The first one to disappear was Conrad, Josef's cousin. Then Jacob's wife. Now Katharina. And in her case we know for sure that she didn't leave voluntarily."

Bastian froze. Marie was right. He had been so jealous, he hadn't understood anything. But all three *had* disappeared—and he had told Margarete, Josef's wife, that she was exaggerating. He sighed and scratched his chin.

"You're right, Marie. Please forgive me. I was beside myself. So what did that whining Wilhelm see?"

Marie smiled and dragged Bastian into the kitchen.

"Wilhelm, could I ask you to tell my husband what happened?"

Wilhelm looked up, and Bastian saw his big, scared eyes.

"It was the Devil. He was tall and black, with a cloak and a hood so deep I could only see his wide jaw. His hands were gigantic. He overpowered Katharina while I was in the cellar, and then me. He tied us to the chairs in the kitchen before we knew what was happening."

Wilhelm burst into tears again, then continued with a faltering voice. "For a long time he didn't say a word. He just stood there in the doorway and stared at us; it felt like an eternity. Then he untied Katharina and threw her over his shoulder. He reeked of so much frankincense. Then he sneaked out of the house like a monstrous shadow, with poor Katharina on his shoulder. The door slammed and he was gone. It was the Devil! I was all alone, and when Huppertz returned . . ."

Another crying spell shook him. Wilhelm sobbed like a child.

"Huppertz is incensed. He says I'm worthless and wants to exclude me from the fraternity. But this brotherhood is all I have in the whole wide world!"

Now he was weeping uncontrollably. Marie gave him a handkerchief.

"Please, Bastian Mühlenberg, you need to help me find Katharina! Please!"

"Now, now—first, calm down, Wilhelm." He couldn't believe a man of Wilhelm's age would be such a crybaby. The last hint of jealousy evaporated when he looked at Wilhelm. Who would be capable of kidnapping three people in such a short period of time? Only one name came to mind: Huppertz Helpenstein! Huppertz owned a black cloak with a hood that could be pulled down deep over his face. Since he went to church regularly, he probably smelled strongly of frankincense. On the other hand, basically every member of the fraternity fit this description. It could have been any of them.

Still, Bastian thought Huppertz was particularly capable of such evil actions. On top of that, he had evidently stolen the gold. His cheeks flushed and hot, Bastian considered his options. Then again, what was Huppertz's motivation? A small voice deep inside him warned Bastian: *Huppertz already has the gold. Why would he make his own wife disappear?*

Bastian shook his head. Maybe the fraternity was too easy a guess, the black cloak too obvious a hint. Who else wore a dark cloak? Conrad! The monk was usually dressed like that. An intense smell of frankincense always lingered inside the monastery. Maybe Conrad had disappeared on purpose? That way, nobody would suspect him of having kidnapped the two women? Maybe he was through with the chaste life of a monk. Once, Bastian now remembered, Conrad had helped his cousin Josef with a foot amputation. He recalled the movements of the monk while he was sawing, how his cloak blew up in the wind and how the sounds of the saw and the bursting of the bones and the inhuman screams of the sick man had almost been too much to endure. Even Josef looked pale, but

Conrad had stayed calm. He'd continued with the same steady rhythm and stayed focused. Indeed, Bastian now remembered vividly, he had looked like the Devil incarnate.

.   .   .

Bastian woke up soaked in sweat. He'd been dreaming. He recognized this dream from before. Now he knew where he had lost the pretty woman with the emerald eyes. It was in the dark labyrinth underneath Zons, and the black Devil was chasing her! Bastian's heart raced.

Trying not to wake Marie, he sneaked out of bed as quietly as possible and tiptoed down the small, steep wooden stairs into the main room of the house, where he lit a candle. He pulled the map of the labyrinth from its temporary hiding place underneath the table. He unfolded the old parchment and let the light of the candle shine over the numerous pathways. Then he opened his notebook and jotted down a number of symbols. Father Johannes had expressly forbidden him to take notes, but a few encrypted symbols surely wouldn't do any harm. Someone would need to decipher his secret code before they could make sense of what they saw. Then he tore the last page out of the notebook and wrote down the corresponding letters for the symbols. This page he would have to guard carefully. Only with these as a guide would someone be able to transcribe his encrypted message.

XII
Present

Anna examined the thin piece of parchment she had found on the floor. She saw a row of letters on the left side, and it seemed the column on the right assigned one specific symbol to each letter. Anna glanced over at Emily, who was sitting on her bed, mumbling to herself. She was still trying to decode the mysterious entries in Bastian Mühlenberg's notebook.

"I'm lost. This might as well be Chinese!" Emily said and sank against the pillows propped up behind her. Anna reached for the notebook entries and compared the symbols with those on the paper she had found. Then she grabbed an empty sheet of paper and began to write.

"What are you doing?" Emily asked.

But Anna didn't answer. She was entranced as she transcribed Bastian Mühlenberg's secret message. When she was done, she looked up at Emily with a broad smile.

"I can tell you exactly what Bastian wrote." She took a deep breath. "There is a labyrinth underneath Zons. Father Johannes had asked Bastian to search for some sort of treasure that was hidden there. Apparently, the place was marked by an image of a double-headed eagle. Once Bastian had retrieved the treasure, Father Johannes hid it in a new place. But Bastian doesn't mention where. He probably didn't want to put it in writing. Here he describes how he descended into the maze. You have to look at this, Emily; it's awesome."

Emily jumped up from her bed and sat down on the floor next to Anna. They had unearthed a forgotten secret. That summer, five hundred years ago, one of the underground alleys had caved in, which had caused the collapse of one of the massive watchtowers that was part of the city wall. Above the alley, a trench had opened up right in front of Bastian's eyes.

In order to better visualize the layout of the maze, Emily and Anna spread out a map of Zons on the dining table. Today's Wiesenstraße followed nearly the same course as what had once been the caved-in alley.

Bastian Mühlenberg had first descended into the labyrinth from outside the city walls. Underneath an old willow tree near the Rhine meadows, he had located a point of access and entered another, parallel aisle that ran underground past the outer ward—which today served as an open-air stage—and the southern border of the city wall before continuing right into the city center. According to his notebook, Bastian had searched for a different access point but found only the one underneath the willow tree. A first glance at the pages suggested that he had discovered something horrible inside the maze, but Anna and Emily decided to transcribe those passages later; first they needed to find the maze.

Bastian had filled many pages with his cryptic messages. The access he had used to descend no longer existed, because the clever city guard had bricked it up that same summer. Anna and Emily looked at each other. Both had the same thought: they had to gain access to the labyrinth. This was the scoop of the century—or make that several centuries! Emily jumped to her feet and ran over to her desk. She returned with a newspaper.

"Read this article, Anna. I assume you heard about the project to renovate the museum courtyard in Zons? Just a couple of weeks ago, a digger almost fell into a pit that suddenly opened up during construction, and they discovered a medieval vault. I bet we'll find access to the maze from the basement of the museum. Just look at the map! The large vaulted alley that Bastian mentions should be right there!"

Emily marked the spot on the map with a thick red cross and pinned it to the wall. The labyrinth consisted of hundreds of narrow, twisted pathways. They'd have to be well prepared if they didn't want to get lost.

.   .   .

Oliver Bergmann walked around the dead woman on the floor of the white-tiled car wash. The body had been squeezed into a hatch on the floor, and now her limbs had stiffened at weird angles, giving her body the surreal look of one of Picasso's cubist masterpieces.

The woman's mouth was open and dark from the blood that had crusted inside it and around her lips. Oliver bent down, squinted, and jumped back when he noticed that the woman's tongue had been cut out and her throat severed. Her eyes were still wide-open with terror. She looked skinny and disheveled. Her wrists and ankles displayed signs of fetters, and in some areas the skin was rubbed raw and covered with bruises.

"Looks as if the perpetrator held her captive for quite some time," Klaus said. He'd arrived late, and Oliver was furious.

"Where the hell have you been?"

Klaus blushed. "I had a date."

Oliver stared at him.

"You know, with Sonja. We made up."

Oliver nodded. It wasn't the first time Klaus and his girlfriend had reconciled after a bad fight. It seemed almost like a game. At least it kept the relationship interesting. The thought of Emily popped in his mind, and he wondered whether they would still be together five years from now. The idea of a future without her made his heart ache.

In the meantime, Forensics had arrived, and the small car wash was packed with people clad in white. Frau Scholten, head of the Crime Lab, squatted down next to Oliver and Klaus and examined the body. With a pair of tweezers, she carefully pulled a small piece of skin that was about to fall off the forearm. It looked wavy and damp but was hardened. She scrutinized the sample under the glaring neon light of the lamps that her staff had mounted in every corner of the car wash.

Frau Scholten raised her eyebrows as she studied the piece of skin from all angles. "I can't say for certain, but it looks as if the body came in contact with acid."

Oliver shot a look at Frau Scholten. He had assumed this all along. "When will you be able to say for certain?"

"Probably an hour, maybe two. Then I'll know whether or not the damage on the skin was caused by chemical burn, and which substance we're dealing with. We can do a quick test."

"Sounds good. Please call me immediately when you have the results. Let's go, Klaus, I want to do some Q&A with Frederick Köppe."

·   ·   ·

Frederick Köppe lived in a tiny attic apartment on Grünwaldstraße, in the heart of the historic city center of Zons. It was unbearably hot and sticky, despite the open window. Oliver glanced at Klaus and saw that his partner's forehead was already drenched in sweat. The two detectives sat down on a stained sofa. Frederick Köppe was very nervous. His left leg wouldn't stop shaking, and Oliver had to fight the impulse to grab it and force him to sit still. Clearly, the guy was hiding something!

"Mr. Köppe, please tell us when and in what capacity you were working for your uncle, Fritz Kallenbach."

Frederick shifted uneasily in his chair. "I'm helping him fertilize the fields, on the big tractor. I do that for lots of the farmers."

His voice was monotonous, and he stuttered. He was obviously mentally challenged, and Oliver almost felt bad for being so judgmental. Then a light *ping* announced that Frederick had received a message on Facebook. Everyone looked over at the computer screen, and Frederick acted even more nervous than before.

"No worries. Do your thing first. We'll wait," Klaus said.

"Oh, no, no, that's OK. Just a friend," said Frederick, staring awkwardly at the floor.

Oliver asked him again: "When was the last time you worked for your uncle?"

"A few days ago. In the mornings, I work at the gate at the chemical plant. In the afternoons I usually help the farmers on the fields, or in the stable."

Oliver inspected the boy closely. The image of the young gatekeeper flashed in his mind. Of course! Frederick was the same guy who had accompanied them on the premises of the chemical plant and disappeared from one moment to the next. Oliver recalled the tense face of Karl Rotenburg, that arrogant publicist whom they had questioned about his missing employee, Markus Heilkamp. There were definitely too many coincidences here.

Oliver glanced at the coffee table. A catalogue caught his attention: it was from Kotte Agricultural Equipment, a manufacturer specializing in manure spreaders. The cover featured their impressive latest model, the ACE XPERT 8700. The tractor-plus-manure spreader resembled a green monster; the catalogue advertised the volume of manure it could spread out in one single go—8,700 gallons. Oliver picked up the catalogue. He had an idea.

"Do you work with this manure spreader?"

"No, the one my uncle owns is much smaller. That one on the cover is the Mercedes-Benz of manure-spreading vehicles. It has four axles and can pump up to almost 3,200 gallons per minute. On the other hand, my uncle says the hoses on his spreader are wider, so we save time because we don't need to liquefy the dung as much."

Fascinated, Frederick Köppe admired the catalogue. Oliver, too, couldn't take his eyes off the green monster with its fat wheels. Wider hoses . . . wide enough for bone fragments to pass through? Oliver concentrated on the detailed description and the images of the machines. His thoughts raced. Several bodies at once could easily fit into a tank as huge as this one. He needed to find out whether the hoses and discharger on Kallenbach's manure spreader were truly wide enough that whole bones from a human foot wouldn't get stuck.

He glanced over at Klaus, who nodded. He had the same idea. He asked, "Herr Köppe, would you mind showing us your uncle's machine? We'd like to take a closer look and also learn how you prepare the manure and how it's transferred into the tank."

Frederick Köppe's face showed both suspicion and excitement. He swayed back and forth until he finally agreed. "I'll show you my uncle's spreader. But keep in mind, it's not the ACE XPERT 8700!"

.   .   .

Oliver Bergmann couldn't comprehend how Fritz Kallenbach's machine was supposedly significantly smaller than the Mercedes-

Benz of manure spreaders they had seen on the catalogue cover. What he saw was pretty huge already. And the smell was huge, too.

They stood in a yard used for storing agricultural equipment, located north of the old Zons city center, and confronted a gray giant equipped with several wide hoses for manure. The closer they came, the worse it reeked. Klaus pulled out a handkerchief and covered his nose.

"What have I done to deserve this?" he said under his breath.

Oliver touched his partner's shoulder and pointed at one of the hoses. "See that diameter? Our bone fragments would comfortably fit through those hoses. I bet you this monster helped scatter them around the fields."

"You could have a point there. Frederick said that his uncle lent the machine to other farmers and that he himself only operates this baby here. I'll call Forensics right away. Maybe they can detect remnants of hydrochloric acid."

Oliver felt satisfied and rubbed his hands together. It was very likely they had solved the question of how the bones had ended up in the field. Yet the most important question remained: Who did it?

Oliver looked around and noticed Frederick standing at the far end of the yard. He was on the phone and visibly upset, waving his arms through the air. It looked like he was having an argument. As Oliver crossed the yard to approach him, he was careful not to step into one of the small piles of dung that dotted the ground. When Frederick noticed Oliver coming closer, he ended the phone call so Oliver wouldn't overhear—obviously a secret conversation.

"Trouble?" Oliver asked.

"Oh, no, that was just my friend," said Frederick and lowered his eyes.

That had not looked like a casual phone call with a friend. Oliver recalled Frederick's frantic reaction when his so-called friend had sent him a message on Facebook. He would need to vet Frederick's Facebook page.

Oliver was burning to question Frederick about his friend, but his instincts told him that he wouldn't get very far. Also, it might not hurt to let the mysterious friend believe he was safe.

"So where's all the manure coming from?" Oliver was certain that Frederick had operated the manure spreader on the days the bone fragments had been scattered. But that didn't explain who had put the bodies into the tank. Oliver didn't think Frederick capable of acting by himself. Either he was completely innocent or he'd followed someone's orders. And that someone had to be his "friend." Oliver sensed a familiar prickling in his gut. He always got that feeling when he was on to something.

Frederick opened the gate of a large barn. They crossed through the barn and reached a second yard, where several big containers were mounted in the ground. Frederick pointed to the container at their feet.

"These are the manure containers. I pump the manure directly into the tank from here. The machine makes it easy."

"And how does the manure get into these containers?"

"I don't know. You'll have to ask my uncle."

Oliver wondered if Fritz Kallenbach was responsible for the bone fragments after all.

"If I understand correctly, you pump up everything that's inside these containers into the tank of the spreader?"

"Yep."

"Do you check the manure when it's delivered?"

Frederick began fidgeting again. *He knows exactly what I'm talking about,* Oliver thought and reminded himself to play it cool. He gave Frederick his broadest, most innocent smile, hoping it would gain his trust. Apparently, it worked. Frederick seemed to relax.

"No, I don't check anything."

Oliver could almost smell the lie. Yet he gave a nod, pretending to be convinced.

"Well, I'm afraid we've come for nothing, then. Let me thank you for all your time and efforts, Herr Köppe. I'll let you go now. Our colleagues from Forensics will stop by in a little while, but it's just a formality. You have nothing to worry about. You know how it is with our bureaucracy—everything follows strict protocol."

He flashed his friendly smile again, shook Frederick's hand, and said good-bye. Frederick let out a huge sigh of relief and hurried away without looking back.

Oliver took out his phone and called Hans Steuermark.

"We need a search warrant, fast. I believe we know how the killer disposed of the bone fragments. And we have a suspect!"

.   .   .

Anna stared at her GPS, annoyed. This was the third time it had sent her in the wrong direction. She was driving in circles, and it was making her crazy. She looked at the time. It was past 7:00 p.m. already. She was running late.

Her phone rang. *Oh, Jimmy,* she thought, *don't get on my nerves now. I'm almost there.*

"Jimmy? Five minutes, OK? My GPS—"

"This isn't Jimmy. This is Matthias Kronberg. I'm sorry, Frau Winterfeld, I didn't mean to disturb you. I only wanted to thank you for your excellent advice—"

Anna heard a clicking noise on the line. "Hello, are you there? Herr Kronberg?" She checked her phone. She had full signal. "Hello?"

"Yes, do you hear me? I just wanted to say thank you and invite you for dinner. Does the end of next week work for you? I'm hosting a dinner party with a few other entrepreneurs and thought it might actually be worth your time—you might meet some new potential clients. I'd like to help spread the word about your excellent service."

Anna thought about it for a moment. "Thank you very much, Herr Kronberg. I'm delighted. Please send me an email with the details."

She ended the call and gave her GPS another dismayed look. Kronberg was starting to drive her nuts, too. He had been calling her every other day, and it almost felt like harassment.

She was lost in Düsseldorf's maze of one-way streets. It was literally impossible to make a left turn. Jimmy lived in Oberkassel, an affluent neighborhood. She had promised to pick him up and go with him to a networking mixer with clients at the Swissôtel, a fancy hotel in Neuss. They would finally have the dinner he'd been pestering her about. Anna hadn't bailed, although she'd much rather spend the evening with Emily. The two friends had decided to descend into the underground labyrinth, and they had loads of prep work to do. It would be a first for both of them. They knew it might be dangerous. Yet it was also Emily's big chance to break into the market for real and establish herself as a serious investigative journalist. Nobody suspected a labyrinth underneath Zons. Discovering it would be a tremendous scoop.

At last Anna parked her car in front of a luxurious mansion. Elegant marble steps led up to an entrance door framed by two large pillars. She scanned the nameplates. There were only four parties. *Not many people for such a big house,* Anna thought. Above the entrance she noticed two security cameras and the red light of an alarm system. She rang the bell and heard Jimmy's crackling voice through the intercom. In the background she heard choral music that reminded her of monks singing Gregorian chants.

Jimmy buzzed her in, and Anna quickly walked up the stairs to his apartment. Above his door, two more security cameras greeted her with their red LEDs. Now she clearly recognized the chanting of monks behind the door. But suddenly, the music stopped and Jimmy opened the door.

Jimmy greeted Anna with a big smile. He had dressed up quite a bit for the occasion. His hair was gelled and shone like wet, black silk. He'd knotted an expensive tie around his neck, and golden cuff links accentuated the sleeves of his white shirt. A fresh cloud of a tangy, masculine fragrance hovered around him; he must have applied it just before he'd opened the door.

Anna looked around the hallway. On the ceiling she spotted two more cameras. Jimmy took her to the living room and offered her a seat. Nervous, she glanced at her watch. Only thirty minutes before the opening speech. They had better hurry.

Jimmy's living room was huge. There was a large fireplace on one side, and, on the opposite side of the room, spanning the entire wall, a long row of windows reaching all the way down to the floor. The lovely old oak parquet added to the exquisite, sophisticated ambience and lent the apartment a sense of welcoming warmth and comfort. When Anna looked up at the ceiling, she saw two more cameras.

"Are you afraid of burglars?" she said to Jimmy, who had just left the living room.

"No, the alarm system was already installed when I took over the apartment, but now I'm actually having a blast with it. I can control it from anywhere, using my laptop or my phone."

Jimmy joined Anna in the living room, finally ready to go. They rushed down the stairs and into Anna's car.

. . .

Anna's cheeks were red and hot. She had downed more than one cocktail with Jimmy and was now calculating how long she'd have to stay before she could drive again. If she remembered correctly, the liver processed one glass of alcohol per hour. That meant she was stuck here for at least two more hours.

Suddenly, she felt a hand on her shoulder and turned around. She was surprised to see Matthias Kronberg. What was he doing here? She didn't remember inviting him. Still, she gave him her most professional smile.

"Herr Kronberg, what a surprise! What are you doing here?"

"I could ask you the same. You know, I have so many events that I didn't even realize your bank hosted this one. I must be on every contact list on the planet." He smiled at her.

For the first time, Anna looked at him more closely. Matthias Kronberg's best years were behind him, but she could still see that he once had been a very attractive man. Now he had dark circles under his gray-blue eyes, and his hair was gray. But the silver sideburns gave him a serious and distinguished look, and he seemed in a jolly mood. Anna assumed it was at least partly because the loan had been approved. She spent the rest of the evening talking with Matthias. He was a splendid entertainer and knew how to converse.

Around midnight, she felt sober enough to drive home and began looking for Jimmy. The party was still in full swing, and Anna squeezed her way through the crowd toward the bar, where she had last spotted Jimmy deep in conversation with some blonde woman. When she didn't see him there, she looked for him at the other end of the room. Jimmy was nowhere to be found.

So typical, Anna thought and pictured him living it up in one of the Swissôtel's many beds. To her surprise, she felt a pang of jealousy. She didn't really care for Jimmy—he was far too superficial for her taste—but she couldn't deny that there was a certain chemistry between them. Slightly disappointed, Anna left the party and drove through the night back to Zons. She fell asleep the moment she got into bed.

. . .

Hans Steuermark glowered at his two best detectives. He was not amused. He had just come back from a press conference, where the local media had grilled him about a damaged bridge on the Autobahn A57. A few weeks ago, someone had set a fire underneath the bridge, and now an expert commission had determined that the bridge was at risk of collapsing and needed a complete overhaul. Subsequently, that stretch of Autobahn had to be closed in both directions, which caused chaotic traffic jams for the commuters between Cologne, Neuss, and Düsseldorf. All the country roads were clogged, and people had to take long detours. The Rhine ferry between Zons and Düsseldorf was in high demand, despite the long waiting lines. The entire transport system was on the verge of a breakdown, and the pressure on the police to arrest the perpetrators grew every day. So far, the police didn't have the slightest clue.

The new bone fragments they had recently discovered, plus the female body in the car wash, didn't soothe Steuermark's discontent. While Oliver and Klaus had come up with some promising leads, they still couldn't present Steuermark with any hard evidence.

As always, Steuermark paced his usual route through his office. He wanted as thorough a briefing as possible. The complete autopsy of the woman had come in and confirmed remnants of hydrochloric acid on her skin.

The door to Steuermark's office swung open and his secretary stood in the doorway, smiling. "The victim has been identified," she said in a low voice and handed Oliver a folder.

Oliver skimmed the papers and read the results: "Dorothea Walser. Age twenty-eight, single. She worked as a credit counselor in a bank in Düsseldorf."

"What about the manure spreader?" Steuermark asked.

"Traces of hydrochloric acid were found there as well. However, only inside the tank. Not inside the containers in the yard. All of them were clean." His last words made him grin. "Well, as clean as a container full of dung can be."

Steuermark stopped pacing. "That means the bone fragments were put directly into the tank of the manure spreader, correct?"

"It looks like it."

"Was Frederick Köppe aware of what he was spreading across the fields?"

"We believe he knew. But because of his mental deficit, he's not likely to have acted alone. We just can't prove it. When we questioned him, his reactions were quite suspicious."

Oliver recalled the obvious lie Frederick had told him.

"Well, then, gentlemen, I want you to start investigating Köppe—each and every phone call, all Facebook contacts, and any other online activity. Find out who's behind him." Steuermark glanced at his watch. "Tomorrow at this time I expect you to give me a complete report. And keep in mind that I want tangible results. I don't want to go through another press conference like the one today." He wiped sweat from his forehead. "Oh, and don't forget to visit that residue cemetery on the premises of Dormagen Chemical Works. I want you to find out what's stored there and how well that place is guarded, if at all. And with that, detectives, have a nice day."

.   .   .

On Monday, Jimmy didn't show up at work. Over the weekend, Anna had sent him a few text messages and even tried to call him once, but he had his phone off. She got angry when she imagined Jimmy and that blonde bimbo from the bar spending a romantic weekend together while she sat in Zons, worrying about him. But when his desk was empty on Monday, Anna began to think something was seriously off. No woman on earth would have kept Jimmy from doing his job. He was far too ambitious and addicted to watching the stock prices change every second.

Anna was unsure what to do next. Her first impulse was to call Emily, but then she hesitated. She had whined about her problems over the entire weekend and didn't want to wear out Emily's patience. Dear, industrious Emily, who had prepared their underground adventure almost entirely by herself because Anna simply couldn't focus. Emily had gathered rechargeable outdoor flashlights, breathable clothes, and glow-in-the-dark spray paint with which they could mark the walls of the twisted maze. She had thought of everything.

But Anna was on edge, thinking of Jimmy. She had to do something. Maybe Emily could call her detective-lover. Anna was sure Oliver could find Jimmy in no time. After another round of debating, she finally called Emily.

. . .

Oliver loathed that arrogant jerk. He admired Klaus, chatting with Karl Rotenburg, spokesman of Dormagen Chemical Works, even though Klaus couldn't stand the guy, either.

A small, white company van had transported them to the far end of the property. Now they were inspecting the so-called residue cemetery. The rectangular plot was maybe a mile long, surrounded by a chain-link fence. They walked along a small path among junk and clutter, past large, defunct steel containers, unidentifiable structures, and rusty measuring devices. When they reached the end of the residue cemetery, Oliver spotted a large, black raven. A true scavenger, the bird had descended to pick at the flesh of a dead animal. Oliver tried to determine what kind of animal it might have been. It seemed too large for a rabbit. He took a few steps closer.

There wasn't much left to look at, and it was impossible to identify from a glance at the skeleton what kind of creature it was. But Oliver did wonder how a relatively large animal had managed to cross the high, tightly woven chain-link fence.

He walked back in the direction they had come from and couldn't believe what he saw. Below one of the fence posts, the wire had been cut. It was professionally done. The cut-out section was inconspicuously attached to the rest of the fence, so it could be easily opened and closed like a door, thus allowing for the transportation of bulky materials.

He looked around. Scrapped hydrochloric-acid containers were behind him. Oliver searched the surrounding area for surveillance cameras. All he saw were two cameras at the entrance to the residue cemetery. He quickly walked back to Klaus, who was still engaged in conversation with Karl Rotenburg.

"Are the cameras at the entrance the only two cameras for the entire section?"

Rotenburg fixed Oliver with his arrogant eyes. "Why, of course. That's the only access to the residue cemetery."

Oliver led the two men to the spot with the open fence. All color—and all arrogance—left Rotenburg's face. He looked distressed. Klaus pulled out a small pair of tweezers, which he used to collect tiny red threads that clung to the fence.

"Looks like our suspect wore red clothing," he said with a deadpan expression while he stored the threads inside a small plastic bag. Then he whispered into Oliver's ear, making sure Rotenburg couldn't understand him: "Wasn't Frederick Köppe wearing a red sweater when we questioned him?"

Oliver nodded. He remembered the old-fashioned red sweater, because it had seemed like a poor choice for a summer's day.

"We should arrest him. We have enough for a warrant."

Oliver shook his head. "I know. But we would only alert the real culprit. I have another idea. We leave everything as is and position two cops here who can observe the section day and night. We might catch him or them in the act, and if we're lucky, our man won't be alone. Do you think anyone can carry those things by himself?" Oliver pointed at the hydrochloric-acid containers.

Klaus nodded. "It's a deal."

. . .

Bingo, Oliver thought. He put down the receiver and leafed through the binder containing the names of the three missing males still considered possible victims.

Peter Schreiner
Markus Heilkamp
Peter Hirschauer

The lab analysis hadn't yielded a match for the first bone fragments, but they had a match for the bones from Kallenbach's field. With a thick red marker, Oliver crossed out the first two names and highlighted the last in neon green: Peter Hirschauer, the successful banker.

Oliver had had a gut feeling about Hirschauer all along, especially after the body of the first banker, Dorothea Walser, had showed up. Now they were probably dealing with two dead bankers; after all, it seemed unlikely that Hirschauer was still alive, what with fragments of his foot bones being scattered across fields.

He opened his laptop and got on Facebook. He typed Frederick's name in the search field and looked at the young man's profile picture. Blond-haired, green-eyed Frederick smiled at Oliver. Whoever had taken that photo had managed to portray Frederick at his best.

Oliver's phone rang. He was happy to see Emily's name on the display and answered. Her voice made him think of her bright smile, and he longed for her embrace.

"Hey, sweetie, it's so good to hear your voice," he said.

"Actually, I wouldn't want to bother you with petty stuff because I know you're swamped, but Anna's worried about a coworker, and I promised her I'd talk to you."

"No worries. Anything that distracts me from my work is welcome, especially when it's coming from you. What's up?" Oliver smiled.

"This past Friday, a coworker and friend of Anna's disappeared during a networking mixer and hasn't shown up since. He's an obsessive investment banker who would never miss a day at work. His name is Jimmy Henders. Would you be able to find him?" Emily paused. "You should know that he's popular with the ladies. My personal take on this is that he's just having a good time. When Anna last saw him at the mixer, he was flirting with a well-endowed blonde over cocktails."

"Okay, I'll take note of his name," Oliver said. "Where was the mixer held?"

"At the Swissôtel in Neuss."

Oliver wrote down the information and hung up. He put aside his notebook and concentrated again on Frederick Köppe's Facebook page. To his surprise, Frederick had more than two hundred friends. Slowly, Oliver scrolled through the list of friends, but he couldn't find any matches with the names on his list of missing people. This seemed like an innocent mix of online friends.

Klaus stormed into the office carrying a large magnetic whiteboard. A box full of markers slipped out of his grip and clattered to the floor. "Hey, buddy, I might need a hand here in a minute." Klaus began to mount the board on the wall.

"What's going on?" Oliver was annoyed. While he was toiling away in the office, trying to find some sort of hint to the puppet master behind Frederick Köppe, Klaus had been shopping. Or so it seemed.

"That's our new whiteboard!" Klaus beamed. Then he took a black marker out of the box and drew several columns on the board.

Oliver was losing it. "How about you actually help me with our current investigation instead of buying school supplies."

"But I *am* helping! This board will significantly improve our communication. Better communication will help us solve the cases considerably faster. Visualizing my thoughts always inspires me."

Oh man, what kind of personality-development seminar did you attend? Oliver thought. When he wanted to communicate, he spoke, and when he wanted to take notes, he'd grab his notebook. But Klaus's euphoria was like a balloon that was impossible to deflate. Klaus didn't pay much attention to Oliver and stoically continued drawing lines on the board. Then he wrote down the names of the missing persons, including the confirmed victim, Dorothea Walser.

Oliver felt anger boiling inside him. That wasn't news to him! The same names were already neatly arranged in his notebook and were all crossed out except one.

Oliver rose from his seat, grabbed a red marker, and crossed out the names he had already eliminated from his own list. Following a sudden impulse, he grabbed a blue marker and added the name *Jimmy Henders* to the list on the whiteboard. Klaus grinned at Oliver, took the blue marker from him, and added two more names.

"Where did you get these names?" Oliver asked, confused.

"I could ask you the same thing!" said Klaus.

Oliver added headings to each column: *Occupation* and *Missing Since*. Once that was done, he completed Jimmy Henders's info.

Name: Jimmy Henders
Occupation: Banker
Missing since: Friday, June 22, 2012

Defiantly, he glanced at Klaus, who didn't waste any time adding the respective information to the other two new names.

Name: Jörg Plaggenwald
Occupation: Banker
Missing since: Friday, June 15, 2012

Name: Kerstin Hohenstein
Occupation: Banker
Missing since: Friday, June 8, 2012

To their combined bewilderment, they realized that all three persons had disappeared on a Friday—which was the second similarity they shared.

"So tell me now, where did you get these names?"

"I did more than shopping, Oliver. I also drove past the lab. They had just finished the DNA analysis and told me they had discovered two matches."

. . .

They had found her much faster than he had anticipated. He realized he shouldn't have left the car wash in such an agitated state. He should have taken the body with him. Then he could have disposed of her as he had done with the others. He furiously whipped his bare back with his cat-o'-nine-tails. *How could you act so irresponsibly?*

I know. I know. Had I gotten rid of her, they wouldn't be right on my heels—but what was I supposed to do?

He flogged his skin yet again. Thin, light-red trickles of blood ran down his back and dropped onto the towel under his knees. The church bells chimed. He distinctly heard their bright sound even through the pain. He glanced at the clock. The time had come.

He rose to his feet and opened the chest with the golden sickle. He took the weapon in his hands and let his index finger run over its sharp blade. Then he walked over to one of the camera screens and zoomed in on his next victim. The bleeding, manacled man in the trunk of the car he'd bought specifically for him looked like a giant embryo. He hadn't regained consciousness. That was too bad, but he would have to amend his punishment anyway. He couldn't return to the car wash, and he didn't have time to find a good alternative.

You'd better split, whispered a voice in the back of his mind.

Don't be a chicken, said a stern, croaking voice from somewhere else. *You only have three more sinners to punish. They won't catch you anytime soon. You have all the time you need. God is with you. And when the work is done, you'll disappear.*

·   ·   ·

Anna and Emily hid in the stalls of the museum bathroom. Their plan was to stay there until after the museum closed and then sneak down into the cellar. Over the past couple of days, Emily had investigated further and discovered a connection between the cellar and the construction area in the courtyard—precisely where they had discovered the medieval vault. Emily hoped that, once inside the vault, they would find a means to access the labyrinth. She was incredibly excited and could hardly wait. This morning she had revised large parts of her new feature series, "The Reaper of Zons," about the medieval serial killer with his golden sickle. Now she couldn't wait to track down the archbishop's treasure. That would clearly be the highlight of her story.

The sound of shuffling steps alarmed her. The steps came closer. Concerned, she glanced over at Anna and gave her a look that said, *Please, don't let them find us!* Someone opened the door to the women's bathroom. The steps crossed past the sinks. A window was closed. The steps receded. Anna and Emily exhaled in relief.

Twenty minutes after closing, they geared up for their adventure. They hadn't heard any sounds for a while and assumed everybody had left. They waited another five minutes and sneaked out of the bathroom. Emily had memorized the layout of the museum and moved with such ease through the dark hallways that Anna had difficulty following her. But in no time they made it down into the cellar, where it smelled damp and musty. Old exhibit props and sets were wrapped in drop cloths. The light from their flashlights darted over the cellar floor.

Emily paused. "I believe it's here." The flashlight illuminated the map. She pointed at a red cross, then walked three steps to the left and stopped in front of a rusted metal door covered in cobwebs. She tried to pull up on the door's lever, but it didn't budge.

"Anna, I need your help. This thing is so rusty it won't move."

But even their joint efforts were unsuccessful.

"It won't work like this. Maybe the lever needs to be unlocked first?" said Anna and shone her flashlight over the door. She carefully felt along the inside of the lever, and her fingers encountered a tiny latch. She pushed it down and heard a faint click.

Elated, Emily tried the lever again, and this time she could easily pull it up. The door opened. Out of the darkness came a gust of cold, damp air. Emily shone her flashlight at the map.

"Nah, we need to go deeper. This is just another cellar room."

She illuminated an iron plate in the floor, about ten feet square. Emily had brought a crowbar and managed to lever the plate a little.

By the time she and Anna finally removed the plate, they were both sweating. But their work was well worth it. After inching the heavy plate to the side, little by little, the flashlight shone on rough-hewn stone stairs that led farther down. Emily looked at Anna triumphantly. There were, indeed, underground alleys. This small, medieval town guarded many ancient secrets that were waiting for her to reveal them. She loved it. She hugged Anna, who was also flabbergasted and awestruck.

Emily was careful as she descended the slippery, narrow stairs. Anna followed her with more fear and trepidation than her ever-enthusiastic friend.

At the foot of the stairs, Emily pulled out an aerosol can and sprayed a large neon cross on the wall.

"So we won't get lost," she whispered.

"Shouldn't we use a rope or something to keep track of the route?" Anna asked.

"No! We don't live in the Middle Ages."

XIII
Five Hundred Years Ago

Bastian had studied the map for hours—not only to find an entrance to the maze but also in order to avoid getting lost once he'd found his way down. Now he was working the ground with a spade and hoe at a spot outside the city walls. He was soaked in sweat and breathing heavily. The exhaustion made his arms and legs tremble, but he wouldn't give in. He was sure that sooner or later he'd discover a point of access underneath the old willow tree. The tree stood close to one end of the trench that had suddenly opened up before him.

He was annoyed with himself for not having investigated the cause of the strange trench sooner. But the mysterious disappearances and his new mission from Father Johannes had taken precedence. When he saw the map of the underground maze, everything made sense. The trench had to be just above one of the many alleys indicated on the map. That alley must have caved in and subsequently caused the watchtower to fall.

Father Johannes had strictly forbidden Bastian from mentioning a single word about the labyrinth to anyone. That was why the citizens and the town's master builder were handicapped as they looked for reasons for the collapse of the mighty tower and the formation of the long trench. Evidently, everyone was at a loss—but the secret of the underground maze had to be protected at all costs, since the wrong people could use the labyrinth to sneak past the customs office and the strong city walls.

Once underground, Bastian took a long rope out of his satchel and attached it to a wooden post that he had fixed in a crack between two rocks. As he advanced deeper into the labyrinth, the rope would gradually unfurl and serve as his orientation, ensuring he'd find his way back. The aisle was very low and narrow. Bastian ducked so his head wouldn't hit the rocky ceiling.

He had wanted to bring Wernhart along, but Father Johannes had insisted Bastian go alone. He was not to speak to anyone about it. If something were to happen to him, nobody would ever find him down here. This realization made him queasy.

He lit a torch. The bright light chased away the sinister shadows, and he felt protected. As he made his way down the narrow path, he counted his steps and stopped when he got to one hundred and fifty. If he had counted correctly, and if he hadn't made any mistakes when practicing above ground the previous day, he was standing right underneath the southern wing of the city wall.

Before he turned into a wider aisle that, according to his calculations, should lead him directly under the marketplace after three hundred large steps, he hammered another wooden post into another crack between the rocks and fixed the rope around it.

Suddenly a jarring scream cut through the silence.

Oh dear God, he was not alone. How was this possible? He tried to listen, despite his agitated state. Latin words echoed from the dark walls and hovered through the labyrinth. The words formed a melody that Bastian vaguely remembered having heard before.

Abruptly, the chanting stopped and there was the sound of a whip hissing through the air. Then he heard the frightened, frail voice of a man trying to speak, but his words were muffled. Bastian couldn't comprehend what the man was saying, but it was clear he was begging for mercy. Bastian thought he recognized the voice. Then a sudden, suffocating coughing spell interrupted the pleading, and he froze in shock. *Heinrich!*

Both terrified and furious, Bastian dropped the torch and, with powers unknown to him, began to run. Several times his head bumped against the low ceiling, but he ignored the stabbing pain and focused only on the direction from where his brother's voice seemed to come. The passage ended, and Bastian slammed into the stone wall with all his force and tumbled to the floor. But he quickly composed himself and rose to his feet. He heard Heinrich's voice much clearer now. Bastian sneaked through a small gap and peeked around the corner of the next pathway.

He couldn't believe what he saw.

XIV
Present

Anna and Emily were standing underneath the museum courtyard. Bastian's notebook entries suggested that somewhere here he had made a horrific discovery, but Emily couldn't decipher the significance of the drawing of what seemed to be a medieval chair.

A few yards ahead of them, a shadow scurried through the darkness. Emily froze, and Anna almost let out a scream. Emily raised the flashlight with a trembling hand, but it didn't help much. The dark alley stared back at them, empty and silent.

"Emily, what was that huge shadow? I'm sure someone's down here. We're not alone."

With wide eyes, Emily looked at Anna. She almost followed her instinct to run back to where they'd started, but her mind commanded her to stay calm. "Anna, are you sure?"

Anna nodded vigorously, her face contorted in fear. She could have sworn she had seen something. *Someone.* "Please, let's turn around, Emily. I don't like this at all."

Another shadow scurried past them—but this time, Emily reacted quickly and shone the flashlight on a big, fat rat scuttling along the wall, where it disappeared through a crack.

"Rats," said Emily. "I hate rats."

Still agitated but somewhat relieved, Emily and Anna took a few deep breaths. After a while, Anna gathered her courage and said, "Let's go on. The rats won't hurt us."

Emily nodded and handed Anna a small aerosol can.

"Here, take this. It's pepper spray. You know, just in case."

Before they continued, Emily sprayed another neon cross on the wall. A surprising breeze blew through the claustrophobic passageways. Its spooky hissing sounded like a ghost wafting through the maze. Emily felt the hair stand up on the back of her neck. After a few yards, they turned right and sneaked through a small gap. This had to be the place. And indeed, there was the chair that Bastian had drawn in his notebook. Anna, who had followed Emily, shrieked again.

This wasn't a chair. It was a monster. Rusty iron nails stuck out from the arms and legs.

"It's a torture device," said Anna. "I saw something like it in a museum a few years ago."

Emily got closer to the chair and stumbled over a clay jar. It clanked as it toppled over.

"What's that?"

XV
Five Hundred Years Ago

In a room sparsely lit by two candles, Heinrich was shackled to a big chair, his arms and legs bound by iron clamps. His shirt was ripped open, and Bastian recognized the necklace Heinrich was wearing—the family amulet, depicting a golden mill on a silver background.

Then suddenly, Bastian's poor brother emitted a horrible scream. A golden sickle whizzed through the air and severed his throat. Heinrich's eyeballs rolled up and his head flopped back. He was dead in an instant.

"No!" Bastian yelled and stormed toward the man in the black cloak. He meant to grab the cloth and knock the evil creature to the ground, but Heinrich's killer simply slid the cloak off his shoulders and ran into the darkness, with a furious Bastian on his heels.

"Conrad, stop! I know it's you!" he yelled, panting, into the blackness. He tried to follow the man a while longer but soon lost him. *Damn it!* The killer must have slipped into one of the many side corridors. Bastian turned around and ran back. The echo of running steps thundered all around. Bastian stormed into another corridor, only to be greeted by emptiness and utter silence. His enemy had vanished.

Bastian had lost his bearings. His heart was beating so fast he was afraid he'd pass out. *Focus, Bastian,* he told himself. *You memorized the entire map. You'll find your way back!*

Gradually, his pulse slowed down and his memory returned. He stumbled through endless corridors for what felt like an eternity, until he finally spotted a faint light ahead. *That must be the place where Heinrich was murdered.* All the fury and adrenaline that he had harnessed to pursue the killer now left his body in a rush, allowing grief to take its place. Tears streamed down his face. *Had I arrived just a minute earlier, Heinrich might still be alive.*

How could he keep the citizens of Zons safe when he wasn't even able to rescue his own beloved brother? How had Heinrich ended up here? When Bastian reached the vault, another horrible surprise awaited him. Heinrich's body was gone, and the wooden chair was empty. *How could this be?* He moved toward the chair and stumbled over a clay jar, falling and hurting his knees on the rough, sharp stones of the vault floor. The jar had toppled over and a thick, reddish liquid was trickling out.

A bestial, pungent smell emanated from the jar. Bastian put the jar upright and looked inside. At first he didn't recognize anything. He shook the jar and held it at an angle. A bloody lump of raw meat slid out and splashed to the floor. Good Lord, what was that? Appalled and disgusted, Bastian turned his head before forcing himself to examine it. Suddenly, he knew what it was. The lump of meat was a tongue. A human tongue. Cramps gripped his stomach and he vomited violently, heaving over and over until nothing more could come out. His skin was cold and drenched in sweat. Again he heard the last jarring screams of his brother and, from before that, his indecipherable, pleading sounds. That devil had cut out Heinrich's tongue!

Bastian flipped the jar over, and three more tongues flopped to the ground with a terrible smacking sound. The two smaller ones must have belonged to women. This sudden realization paralyzed Bastian. Katharina, and old Jacob's wife! These were their tongues, for sure! A million thoughts raced through Bastian's head, and a new question rose like a sinister, menacing cloud on the horizon: *Whom did the fourth tongue belong to?*

XVI
Present

Emily gently held the brittle clay jar in her hands. "It's mind-boggling that this jar has never been discovered," she said, and looked at Anna. "According to the manuscript you deciphered, this is the place where Heinrich Mühlenberg, Bastian's older brother, was murdered. Bastian never found the body. The killer chained the victims to this chair, cut out their tongues, and tortured them for several days before he finally severed their throats with a golden sickle. The tongues were supposed to represent their lies, their deadly sins—and he collected them inside this jar. Isn't it horrific?" Emily handed the jar to Anna.

"No, thanks, I don't need to touch that thing. Don't you want to take some photos of the chair? You'll need them for your article!"

Emily took a few pictures, and the glaring flash flickered through the darkness.

Anna thought she spotted that spooky large shadow a few more times. She could almost feel "the Reaper" holding a sharp sickle against her throat, ready to sever it in one smooth cut. Yet everything seemed quiet.

Emily decided she had taken enough pictures of the torture device. Without the illuminating flashes from the camera, this once-hellish courtyard was again transformed into just a narrow underground corridor hewn into stone, where the air felt sticky and had a musty smell. Emily opened the map and shone her flashlight on it. She ran her fingers over a few of the lines, trying to determine their location.

"Archbishop von Saarwerden's treasure was hidden near the Juddeturm. Heading north, this corridor here should take us there." She folded the map, stowed it in her bag, and marched in the indicated direction. Anna followed close behind. Drops of sweat beaded on her brow.

After about fifty yards, Anna stumbled over a sharp stone and fell. Her knee bled, and she moaned. Emily pulled a can of liquid bandage spray out of her bag and treated the wound. Emily was so focused on Anna's wound that she forgot to hold tightly to the flashlight, and it fell to the ground and rolled out of sight.

"Damn it!" Emily felt around her. "Anna, can you please give me some light over here? I think that's where it is." But even with the bright beam from Anna's flashlight, Emily didn't find it. Instead, a pile of rocks caught her attention, for the stones were arranged in such a distinct pattern that it seemed deliberate. Limping closer, Anna spotted Emily's flashlight at the base of the pile. Emily came forward and squatted down. The flashlight was stuck, but when she pulled with greater force, she managed to retrieve it from underneath the stones.

Suddenly, a low rumble filled the corridor. It wasn't particularly loud, but Emily picked up on it. The sound seemed strange. She looked long and hard at the rocks, some of which were rolling and sliding downward.

"These rocks are covering something." She hesitated and took a deep breath. "Actually, this pile reminds me of a stone grave." She set out to remove the rocks.

"Are you saying that this is the place where the archbishop's treasure was hidden?"

"No, Bastian Mühlenberg doesn't mention this spot at all. The treasure was farther north. We only walked fifty yards, if that."

Emily got busy removing stones. Suddenly, her hands brushed against something. "Anna, please hold both flashlights and shine them here. I found something."

The twin beams illuminated the thing in Emily's hand and she immediately recognized what it was. She dropped it to the ground with a loud shriek.

The dry, brownish skeleton of a human hand lay before them.

XVII
Five Hundred Years Ago

Bastian was still squatting in front of the inert, bloody tongues. The disgusting, almost-sweet smell of human decay clouded his brain. Both grief and anger simmered in his chest, and he didn't notice the shadow sneaking up behind him.

After a forceful blow to the back of the head, everything whirled and went black. At the last moment, he managed to roll to the side and avoid the next blow that slammed into the ground. Bastian moaned and rose to his feet. Staggering, he faced his opponent, who was geared up to strike again. Bastian managed to jump behind his attacker, who stumbled and hesitated, not knowing what to do next.

Bastian took advantage of this moment of weakness, wrapped his strong arms around the man's throat, and squeezed with all his might. He thought of his dying brother and squeezed even tighter. He felt the man's resistance growing weaker and heard him wheezing. His adversary was desperately gasping for air and jabbed his elbows into Bastian's sides. But Bastian didn't feel any pain. Without mercy, he closed his arms around the killer's throat until the man passed out. *You devil! You shall burn in hell!* Bastian thought as he let the unconscious body drop.

Blind with rage, Bastian sat on top of the man and hammered his fists against the man's chest. He ripped the black cloak off his head, sure he'd be staring Conrad in the face. But Bastian was startled to find himself looking into the face of Brother Ignatius. He jumped up, electrified. How was this possible? How could Bastian not have noticed what the monk had been up to all along?

I've just visited your brother Heinrich. He seems to be doing much better. The words cut through Bastian's memory like a sword. He looked at Brother Ignatius's massive hands. How often had he wondered why a monk would have strong hands like these? Overcome with leaden sadness, he shook his head. *Heinrich, please forgive me. I'm so sorry I didn't come to your rescue earlier. I could have saved you.*

Could you really, Bastian? a tender voice asked deep inside him. *You know full well how sick he was.*

Yes, but he didn't deserve to die like this. Tears streamed down Bastian's face. He had to find his dear brother's body. At least he could comply with Heinrich's last wish and bury him in the cemetery of Knechtsteden Abbey.

He cut off a long length from the rope he was carrying and maneuvered the monk's heavy body onto the torture chair. Immediately the nails bore deep into Brother Ignatius's flesh, and he moaned, instantly fainting again. Bastian enclosed the monk's hands and feet inside the iron clamps with the same fetters that had bound his brother. *I want this bastard to suffer the same pain he inflicted upon Heinrich,* Bastian thought with gratification. Then he slipped away to find his brother.

Bastian reasoned that Heinrich's body couldn't be that far. Brother Ignatius hadn't had much time to hide the body. Bastian searched the aisles to the east. He found nothing but darkness. He returned to his starting point and headed north. With his torch he thoroughly lit every corner of the corridor, but all he saw were rats scurrying away and bats hanging from the ceiling. Just when he was about to turn around, he noticed a pile of stones ahead. His heart began to pound faster. The closer he came, the more the unmistakable smell of decay grew. Overcome with nausea, he grabbed a corner of his jerkin and covered his nose. He stopped in front of the stone pile. The smell was unbearable. A swarm of flies hummed around his head. Worms were creeping out of the shadows. Bastian kicked aside a fat, dead rat. Determined, he began to remove the stones from the makeshift grave until he had unearthed all the bodies. He recognized Katharina, Huppertz's wife; old Jacob's wife; and Brother Conrad. How much wrong had Bastian done that poor man in his thoughts!

Only Heinrich's body was missing. Bastian tried to remove another set of stones, but he realized he had already dug as deep as he could.

Damn it, where was his brother's body?

XVIII
Present

"Oh my God, a dead body," Anna said, still shining the flashlight's bright rays onto the remains of the human hand. "We need to call the police—now!"

She was having trouble breathing and sat down on the rocky floor. Even Emily looked pale and scared.

"Anna, do you think this is connected to the shadow we thought we saw a while ago?" She sank down next to Anna, who was inspecting the hand. *This hand looks mummified,* Emily thought.

"Do you smell anything, Emily?"

"No, why?"

"Because if it doesn't smell like decay, it means the body is pretty old. Actually, look at the hand. There's no tissue left, only bones. It must be *very* old."

Staring at the hand bones, Emily inhaled deeply. There wasn't the slightest hint of decay, and, after the first shock, it was plain to see that the bones were very brittle. With all the courage they could muster, Emily and Anna began to remove one rock after the other and slowly unearthed an entire skeleton. When they had almost finished, they examined it closer. The chest was barely recognizable, as the heavy stones must have smashed the rib cage. Something glittered when the beam of Emily's flashlight shone on it. She bent down and pulled a necklace with a golden amulet from between the bones. The amulet carried the image of a mill. Emily couldn't believe her eyes and took a deep breath.

"Anna!" she whispered. "I think we might have found Heinrich Mühlenberg!"

XIX
Five Hundred Years Ago

Bastian had spent hours searching for his dead brother. He was exhausted and finally gave up, sinking down on the hard ground. His torch was almost out and threw only a faint light onto the walls of the maze.

He sighed with despair and leaned back against the cold stones. He felt for his amulet and pulled it out from under his shirt. When they were born, his father had given each of his six sons such an amulet. To the casual observer the amulets looked identical, but they differed in the position of the wings of the mill. With each newborn son, the old Zons miller had asked the goldsmith to slightly turn the wings. The ones on Bastian's amulet resembled a cross, the wings standing at straight right angles.

Bastian let the amulet slip underneath his shirt again and reached into the left pocket of his pants. He pulled out a small golden statue of the Virgin Mary. During his frantic search he hadn't found Heinrich, but he had found what he had come for in the first place: he had secured the archbishop's secret treasure. The statue had lain in the exact spot indicated on the map, right underneath the Juddeturm. The many precious stones adorning the statue sparkled in the fading light of the torch. Bastian examined the statue from all sides, but he didn't see an opening. Did this little figurine really contain Archbishop von Saarwerden's miraculous remedy?

Disheartened, he slipped the statue back into his pocket. He didn't need the cure anymore. Even if he disobeyed Father Johannes's words, he couldn't heal his brother's lung ailment anyway. Bastian shook his head. Again, his brother's jarring, desperate scream cut through his memory. Wrath like poisonous bile rose inside him. *Damn it. Brother Ignatius, that devil.* He would make him confess where he'd hidden his brother's body.

He jumped to his feet, ran over to the torture device, and brutally shook Ignatius, but the monk didn't come to.

"I'll take you to the dungeon and make you talk, you bastard!"

XX
Present

"How do you know it's Bastian's brother?" Anna asked.

"He's wearing the miller's amulet. Or rather, what's left of it." Emily stroked the edges of the little golden mill. "We'll have to carry his bones out of here and bury him in the cemetery of Knechtsteden Abbey."

"Are you crazy? I'm not touching these bones!"

"I'm sure Bastian Mühlenberg would appreciate it. Especially if you were involved, Anna. You owe him, don't you think?"

Anna's blood rushed in her ears. She thought for a moment. Emily was right. Without Bastian's appearance—or his apparition— several months ago, she would have fallen victim to the copycat killer and his fatal puzzle. On the other hand, she was a banker. She didn't believe in supernatural phenomena, only in facts. And dead meant dead. She had long questioned her sanity for being so convinced that she had actually met Bastian Mühlenberg in real life.

A soft breeze caressed her cheeks and she felt the hair stand up on the back of her neck. Where could such a breeze come from in this dank cellar?

"Okay, then. Let's get him out of here."

Anna set out to free the skeleton from the remaining rocks. She applied all her strength to remove a particularly heavy rock, but it wouldn't budge. Emily joined forces with her, and only when the two women pushed against the rock with all their strength were they eventually able to move it. Everything afterward seemed to unfold in slow motion.

The ground beneath Anna's feet split open. Rocks and dust clouds fell from the walls. She anticipated what was coming, but she was frozen. She couldn't jump to the side, where she would have been safe. Instead, her legs gave in and Anna plunged into the big, black hole that had opened up in front of her. In desperation, she tried to grasp onto the crumbling edge around her, but the stones broke away under her aching fingers, and she slid into the unknown depths. Strangely, the impact was not as brutal as she had feared. Seconds later, Emily fell on top of her, and Anna could feel and hear some of her own ribs crack. She could hardly breathe.

"Are you OK?" asked Emily, slowly rolling off of Anna.

Anna wasn't sure. But she nodded anyway.

"Anna?"

It was so dark Emily didn't see her nodding, so Anna forced herself to press out a coarse "Yes." Her dry throat burned. She carefully touched her ribs and it didn't hurt as much as she had feared. Maybe she only had a few bruises.

"I'll call Oliver. I should have told him about our secret expedition. He'll be so mad at me," Emily said, switching on her flashlight and searching for her phone. She had come to regret their secret mission. On the other hand, Oliver was so busy these days with his new case, and Emily knew for a fact that he would never have allowed her to go had she let him in on her plans. Of course, she was well aware of the risks involved in exploring an unknown, ancient labyrinth alone. But she'd wanted to be the one who made this incredible discovery public.

Anna said, "Let's try and find a way out of here first. I don't feel too bad, really."

Emily shone the flashlight over the stone walls. Their pit was about twenty square feet around and maybe ten feet high. She stretched her arms up. Damn it, it was far too high. She checked her cell phone. No signal. What did she expect down here? She held the phone up high. Still no signal. Standing on her tiptoes, she stretched up as far as she could, and bingo! A reception bar appeared. She struggled to hold the position as she pushed the button to call Oliver's number.

. . .

Dietrich Hellenbruch shifted uncomfortably in his seat. What did these detectives always want from him? One would assume they had more important things to do than stir up his life. He vividly remembered his previous visit to this same precinct in Neuss, several months ago. They had taken the portrait of Marie away from him. It was a small, original oil painting, which he had loved so much. It was from the fifteenth century, depicting Bastian Mühlenberg and his wife. They had confiscated it, and it had taken Dietrich tremendous effort and patience to retrieve it. Marie was the most magnificent woman he had ever laid eyes on. He believed that beautiful women existed only in a faraway past. Nowadays, many women wore short hair, which he found utterly unattractive. And the few who let their hair grow long didn't keep it neat and tidy but left it wild and messy. It was obscene. Marie, however, wore her long, blonde hair in two lovely braids, as was appropriate.

So here he was, back in this ugly precinct. This time around, they were berating him because he had discovered Marie's doppelganger. It was none of their business. And he had only followed her once to her apartment. Just once!

"Herr Hellenbruch. I'm just making sure we're on the same page here. Stalking is a felony. Frau Sandra Schwanengel has filed a complaint against you. You must stop following her."

Detective Bergmann scrutinized the old archivist. Oliver only knew of the stalking incident from a colleague who had mentioned it over lunch. A week ago, Sandra Schwanengel, an undergraduate student who earned money on the side working at McDonald's, had filed a complaint. When Oliver recognized the defendant's name, he immediately had Dietrich Hellenbruch summoned to the precinct.

Hellenbruch's encyclopedic knowledge about the town's history was no doubt brilliant, but something about him didn't sit well with Oliver. He had even been a suspect, if only for a short time, when they were investigating the fatal-puzzle case. And here he was again, sitting across from Oliver and his partner Klaus—and sporting a bright-red sweater, no less. Just like Frederick Köppe's red sweater. Why had Hellenbruch popped up again during their investigation? Could it be merely a coincidence? He glanced at Klaus, who winked back at him. *He saw it, too,* Oliver thought. He would rather have ignored the red sweater, but he couldn't.

"We're done for today, Herr Hellenbruch. But you've been warned. If you continue to harass Frau Schwanengel, she'll file for a restraining order. And you don't want that."

The archivist nodded and stood. As Oliver walked him to the door, he bumped into Hellenbruch and surreptitiously pulled a few fibers from the red sweater. *It's always better to double-check,* he thought. He'd have the lab compare these fibers with the ones they had found on the fence at Dormagen Chemical Works.

. . .

After Hellenbruch left, Oliver returned to his office and stared at the five names written in big red letters on the whiteboard:

PETER HIRSCHAUER
Status: missing
Bone fragment 5A.2 matched

DOROTHEA WALSER
Status: murdered
No bone fragments matched

JIMMY HENDERS
Status: missing
No bone fragments matched

JÖRG PLAGGENWALD
Status: missing
Bone fragment 8A.3 matched

KERSTIN HOHENSTEIN
Status: missing
Bone fragment 7B.1 matched

He sat down at his desk and leafed through the missing-persons folders. Three bank employees had disappeared in June. The first one reported missing was Kerstin Hohenstein. Oliver skimmed the report. She was last seen at a networking mixer that took place at the Swissôtel in Neuss.

A jarring alarm went off inside Oliver's head. Wasn't the Swissôtel the same hotel where Jimmy Henders, Anna's coworker, was last seen? Oliver tried to remember the details of what Emily had told him, but he wasn't quite sure. Next he looked at the report for Jörg Plaggenwald. He had disappeared exactly one week after Kerstin Hohenstein. He, too, was last seen at a reception his bank had hosted for their clients. That one had taken place in the Düsseldorf Hilton, but the similarities were startling. He opened Peter Hirschauer's folder. His bank had laid him off before his disappearance, so it was difficult to know the exact day he'd gone missing.

Then Oliver studied the photos that the forensic technicians had taken in Peter Hirschauer's apartment. A picture of his desk caught Oliver's attention. The print was out of focus, so he had to resort to the digital files. He zoomed in on the image. He knew exactly what he was looking for—and bingo, he found it among the papers on the desk. The invitation read:

Association of Rhine County Banks
Monthly Mixer
Presentation of Innovative Financial Instruments
Swissôtel Neuss
April 28, 2012
6 p.m.

Oliver clicked out of the photo and closed the folders. Just to be on the safe side, he pulled out the binder for Dorothea Walser, the woman they had found brutally murdered inside the car wash on Highway B9. She, too, had last been seen at a networking mixer. So Oliver could say with utter certainty that the killer snatched his victims from cocktail receptions hosted by various banks in the area.

The door to his office flew open, and Hans Steuermark entered with decisive steps.

"Where's Gruber?"

"He's instructing the two patrolmen assigned to observe the residue cemetery in Dormagen. We hope our unknown suspect shows up there sooner or later."

Steuermark nodded. "Excellent. Frau Scholten sent over the latest lab results. Apparently they detected traces of gold on Dorothea Walser's body. They believe the killer used a golden, sickle-shaped weapon to cut out her tongue and then sever her throat. The material in question is estimated to be at least three hundred years old, if not considerably older. We've commissioned an expert for further in-depth investigation. It's incomprehensible how such an old blade would cause such smooth, sharp cuts."

Oliver's phone rang, and Emily's name appeared on the display. He debated whether he should call her back later or answer, but his desire to hear her sweet voice was too strong.

Her voice was different than he had expected, sounding far away and shaky. The reception was poor; he could hardly understand her. "Oliver, help us," she said. "We're in the labyrinth beneath Zons!"

A sense of dread overtook him. Something sounded terribly off. "I can barely hear you, Emily! *Where* are you?"

"In the underground labyrinth, with Anna . . . my apartment. There's a map—" *Click.* They were cut off. Oliver immediately called back, but it went straight to voice mail. *Damn it.* He made several more attempts, all of them fruitless. Eventually he gave up. His face was dark red. Steuermark cocked his head and focused his eagle eyes on Oliver.

"What's going on, Bergmann?"

"Herr Steuermark, I'm terribly sorry, but I have to run. My girlfriend's in danger. Please tell Klaus to vet all the guests who were at those networking events where the bank employees were last seen."

Oliver grabbed his coat and left Hans Steuermark in a rare state of speechlessness.

On his way to her apartment, Oliver called Emily every minute, but the phone was dead. *Emily, where the hell are you? I hope you're OK!* His heart beat fast in his throat, and the ride to Cologne took an eternity. Because of the damaged bridge, Oliver was rerouted over the jammed country roads. Even his blue light didn't help. It took over an hour until he finally arrived at the graduate students' dorm. Since the main entrance door opened and closed frequently, getting inside was easy. Oliver didn't have to wait longer than two minutes, when a chubby young woman with greasy hair left the building. Oliver slipped inside and ran up the stairs to Emily's tiny apartment.

Oh no! Standing in front of her door, he suddenly realized he didn't have a key. He examined the thick doorpost and colorful doormat. Maybe she hid an extra key somewhere. He lifted the doormat, but all he saw were dust balls. Then he felt along the upper edge of the door frame. *Got it.* He found the key in the right corner. *She should be more careful,* Oliver thought, but right now that didn't matter.

Oliver looked around. A small bedroom and an even-smaller kitchen led into the living room. Several receipts were piled on the coffee table there. He frowned as he glanced over them. Apparently Emily had fully equipped herself, at some expense, for a major expedition into the unknown labyrinth beneath Zons—and all without telling him. Oliver went into the bedroom and stopped in front of a large city map that was pinned to the wall. Hanging next to the city map was the description of a labyrinth. Apparently there were countless twisted, narrow lanes running underneath Zons. South of the Juddeturm, Oliver spotted a double-headed eagle and an asterisk. According to the explanations in a sidebar, the eagle indicated a secret hiding place for a treasure that had belonged to some archbishop Oliver had never heard of. Another, larger, red asterisk designated the access to the maze. It was located underneath the museum courtyard.

Why hadn't she mentioned anything to him? He knew she was working on her new assignment, about some crazy guy in fifteenth-century Zons who carried a golden sickle and cut out the tongues of people he designated as sinners, eventually severing their throats. A thought flashed in his mind: perhaps Emily's research was somehow connected to his current investigation. But he managed to chase the thought away. He'd deal with his job later.

He studied the map and the notes as thoroughly as possible before he tore them off the wall and shoved them into his pockets. He had no clue how and where he was supposed to find Anna and Emily, but his instincts told him he had better hurry.

.   .   .

Klaus was not amused. Now he had to deal with Steuermark alone, just because Oliver's girlfriend was having issues. Did he really have to drop everything and run? Steuermark was pacing back and forth in front of Klaus's desk like a hungry tiger. How was he supposed to focus on the investigation? Trying to locate each person who had attended all the networking events over the past several weeks was tedious work. But at least he had found a few.

"You need to look for names of people who attended all of the five mixers where bank employees disappeared."

Klaus didn't dare contradict Steuermark and say he was already a step ahead of his boss, though he wanted to. It had been a slow, painstaking chore, especially with Steuermark hovering over his desk, but eventually he had found two names.

"One match is Jimmy Henders. But he's one of the missing bankers. The other match is an entrepreneur—Matthias Kronberg."

"Interesting. Run a background check on both of them."

"On Jimmy Henders, too?" Klaus was puzzled. Had Henders turned into a suspect?

"Yeah, why not. He was the last to disappear. Maybe he abducted the other bankers, and his disappearance is just a ruse. It's a possibility we can't rule out just yet."

Hans Steuermark turned to go, but then thought of something else. "And don't forget to examine their Facebook profiles. I'm sure we'll find something."

Steuermark left, and Klaus was finally alone. *Thanks a lot, Oliver.* Stuff like that was usually his partner's specialty. Furiously, he called Oliver's phone, but it was off. *Fantastic!* Klaus opened his browser and went to work.

.   .   .

Thanks to Emily's excellent research and documentation, Oliver had found the access point to the labyrinth without difficulty. He knew that, as a detective, he shouldn't be breaking into public buildings, but this was an emergency. He was glad that Zons was such a peaceful and safe little town that the museum didn't even have an alarm system.

Inside the labyrinth, the darkness was impenetrable. He pulled out his flashlight and switched it on, and for reassurance, Oliver reached for his Glock. The weapon's weight made him feel safer.

"Emily!" he yelled into the darkness. Faintly illuminated by his flashlight, the blackness around him reminded Oliver of a dark velvet veil. It was cold and damp. He thought it was incredibly brave of Emily to venture into this unfathomable maze. In the company of Anna, who was tough in her own right, Emily was nearly unstoppable.

"Emily!" he yelled again.

Nothing. He heard only his own voice echoing off the walls.

"Oliver . . . ?"

From a distance, fragments of the soft little voice he loved so much reached his ears. However, he couldn't determine the direction from which the voice was coming. The sounds were too faint. He looked at the archbishop's map and ran into a corridor he hoped was the right one. Anna and Emily must have gone that way, too.

Just as he began storming into the darkness, he stopped at the point where two paths forked off. Then he noticed a neon cross on the wall. Why would they have chosen the direction that didn't lead to the treasure? Still, he turned around and followed the mark. One thing was certain: it was the way they had taken.

Oliver kept calling Emily's name. He was lost in the maze of narrow, twisted corridors, and it was hard to determine where her voice was coming from. To make matters worse, he hadn't seen any neon crosses on the walls for maybe fifty yards. Breathing was difficult, and he wiped his sweaty forehead and glanced at the map. It seemed he'd been walking for too long. Maybe he had gone in circles. He pulled out a Kleenex and affixed it to the rocky wall, where he hoped it would be most visible if he should walk past again. Suddenly, a paralyzing fear came over him. What if he never found them? Then he'd order a canine unit. Of course that's what he'd do. The words *Oliver! You'll find them!* became his mantra as he worked his way through the darkness. His flashlight flickered eerily, and here and there Oliver thought he saw movements in the shadows. When he shone his flashlight against the wall, it illuminated a white Kleenex. He froze.

He had turned left the first time. Now he chose the paths to his right. He shouted Emily's name at regular intervals. Each time he heard a dim echo of her voice, but it didn't help. Heading deeper into the labyrinth, he arrived at another fork in the pathways. He affixed another tissue to the wall. As he looked up again, he noticed a human silhouette out of the corner of his eye. His first reaction was to pull his pistol. Something—someone—was there in the dark. Slowly, he put one foot in front of the other. At the corner of the path he saw the movement again.

"Stop! Wait!" Oliver yelled.

The person stopped, then hurried on. The beam of the flashlight wasn't powerful enough, but he caught a glimpse of a tall man with tousled blond hair. The man smiled at him.

"Stop! Police!" Oliver yelled again and shone his light where the man had stood, but he was nowhere to be seen. Oliver was stunned. How could anyone disappear so fast? He shone his flashlight at the walls. He wanted to find a gap that would explain the sudden disappearance. And indeed, right where he had seen the man, he found another, smaller corridor.

"Come out! Police!" he shouted down the corridor.

"We're here, Oliver!"

"Emily? Anna?"

"Yes, we're down here!"

Oliver ran as fast as he could. Now he could hear them loud and clear. He stopped in front of a pile of stones and stared into the hollow eye sockets of a skull. He froze. Then he regained his composure and shone the flashlight beyond the stones and found the pit.

"Emily, Anna—oh my God, are you down there?"

He lay down on his stomach and reached into the abyss. But the pit was too deep, and he couldn't even touch Emily's fingers. Emily pulled a rope out of her backpack and threw it up to Oliver.

Ten minutes later, and drenched in sweat, Oliver had freed Anna and Emily and given Emily the embrace he had longed for. Then he gently pushed her away.

"Damn it, Emily, what the hell were you thinking, scaring me to death like that? You and Anna could have died. Why didn't you say something?"

"I know . . . I'm really sorry. It was so stupid. But I didn't expect it to be so dangerous!"

He could no longer restrain himself. He drew her closer and kissed her, all the anger and fear melting into passion. Emily playfully bit his lips, and he held her even tighter. Eventually she surrendered. Triumph pulsated through his veins.

But where was Anna going? He saw her flashlight in the distance and quickly ran after her. "Anna, come back! I don't think we're alone down here."

Anna didn't turn around. Like a pillar of salt, she stood there and stared into the darkness. "I saw him. I think I'm going crazy."

"Who?"

Oliver touched her shoulder and turned her around. Anna was pale and wobbly. This labyrinth was giving everyone the creeps. He might have loved all kinds of adventure movies, but he preferred them on the big screen, not in real life.

"I saw a man with blond hair. He looked like Bastian Mühlenberg."

"Aw, Anna, that's just the shock," Emily said and gave Anna a hug. "Let's get out of here. I definitely have enough material for my feature."

·　　·　　·

On their way out, they got lost several times before they finally found the exit. They had marked the spot where they'd found the remains of Heinrich Mühlenberg so it would be easy to recover the bones later. As soon as they had passed the last cellar door and were moving along the hallways of the museum, Anna received a text message. She winced when she heard the sound and quickly began searching for her phone in her backpack. The message was from Jimmy.

See you Friday at the Swissôtel? Sorry for not getting back to you earlier.

Anna stopped. "That's so strange. Jimmy just texted me."

Again, an alarm went off in Oliver's head. Why now? A clanking sound disturbed his thoughts. Something metallic had fallen to the ground. Oliver looked around and saw Heinrich's golden miller's amulet on the floor. Emily had shown it to him and he'd brought it along as evidence; it had slipped from his pocket. He took a closer look at the small, golden mill with the silver background. And again he felt this strong inkling. An elusive thought went through his mind. He focused as hard as he could. Then suddenly it came to him.

"Anna, Emily, would you mind coming to the precinct? I need to look at something."

"Sure. My ribs are still aching, but I don't think anything's broken. No point wasting the day in a hospital waiting room."

.   .   .

Less than thirty minutes later, they entered Oliver's office. A brooding Klaus stood in front of the whiteboard. Many red crosses and yellow arrows had turned the whiteboard into an abstract painting. Klaus had circled two names in bright red and added several exclamation points behind them.

"But that's one of my clients!" Anna said, pointing at Matthias Kronberg's name.

Klaus hadn't noticed them and jumped. He looked from Anna to Oliver, who stood right behind her.

"Oh, look who decided to swing by!" Klaus said. "Do you have any idea of the chaos that broke out after you left? I suggest you say good-bye to the ladies and we get to work."

Oliver shook his head. "No. We need them. Trust me."

Klaus raised his eyebrows. He put the marker to the side and sat down in his office chair. "Whatever, just look at the whiteboard and piles of binders. Basically, I solved the case. The only thing missing is the link to Frederick Köppe. I've eliminated all but two suspects, and, well, you can guess who they are." Klaus grinned.

It didn't take much to provoke Oliver. He put the Mühlenberg amulet on Klaus's desk.

"Why don't you explain the link to this little thing here? I wasn't just out there having a good time."

Klaus held the amulet between two fingers and inspected it. "Sweet. I like it. It looks old. We could throw a party if we sold it."

Oliver jerked the amulet from Klaus's hand. "Forget it. I'll get the amulet over to the lab as soon as possible. I bet the gold's as old as the traces of gold from that sickle the killer used to cut Dorothea Walser's tongue out, before . . ." Oliver coughed. "Before he severed her throat."

This connection with the history of Zons had become evident to Oliver when the amulet jangled to the floor on their way out of the maze. In that moment, he remembered Hans Steuermark's monologue about the lab results for the murder weapon. He would have never imagined that yet another sick copycat killer would live out his ugly fantasies by rehashing the past of small-town Zons. Hadn't the fatal puzzle been enough?

Klaus whistled through his teeth and grinned. "Well, now all we need is an expert in medieval murder weapons from our county— but particularly from Zons?" He looked expectantly at Emily. She was very pale, but nevertheless she launched into an exhaustive explanation.

"Cultures as early as the Celts used a golden sickle as a ritual instrument. The Celtic priests were known as druids. The druids would use a golden sickle to cut the mistletoe from oak trees. Another famous ritual was the sacrifice of the bull, where a golden sickle was used as well. Roughly five hundred years ago, a monk in Knechtsteden Abbey had a golden sickle made just for him. The sickle represented truth and purity. To make their sins visible, he cut off the tongues of people he had identified as liars. Afterward, he killed them by severing their throats. His name was Brother Ignatius, and he became known as the Reaper of Zons. Apparently, he gave his victims a chance to atone when they came to see him for confession. But when they didn't follow the penance he ordered, or if they tried to buy one of the popular indulgence letters in order to rid themselves of their sins, he killed them. Not doing penance was a lie, a deadly sin, in his eyes, and that's how he justified the murders—until Bastian Mühlenberg put a stop to his ludicrous game. The golden sickle remained with the monastery, but the body of Heinrich, Bastian's brother, who also fell victim to the Reaper, was never found. That is, until Anna and I located it today in the underground labyrinth beneath the museum."

Oliver looked at Emily with admiration.

"What you're saying is that it's possible the sickle has reappeared and that our killer has been playing Brother Ignatius's sick game?" Klaus asked.

Oliver frowned and quickly skimmed some of the binders on Klaus's desk. "None of our victims were particularly religious. I don't see those bankers going to confession," he said. Then he went to his laptop and opened a browser. "What would be the modern equivalent of buying an indulgence letter? Maybe our victims have committed a modern deadly sin." He searched for "seven deadly sins" and clicked on the Wikipedia page. From there he clicked a link to a list of "seven social sins" according to Mahatma Gandhi.

The Seven Social Sins of the Modern World
1. Wealth without Work
2. Pleasure without Conscience

3. Knowledge without Character
4. Commerce (Business) without Morality (Ethics)
5. Science without Humanity
6. Religion without Sacrifice
7. Politics without Principle

As soon as he read the first sin, Oliver felt that familiar tingle. *Wealth without work.* Banks earn money with money, not with work. This would explain why all the victims were bankers. He printed the page with the seven modern sins, highlighted the first line, and put the paper on the whiteboard with a magnet.

Klaus stood and walked over to the board. "As I said, I've vetted the patrons of all the pertinent networking events. There are only two people who attended all the receptions where our victims were last seen: Matthias Kronberg, an entrepreneur, and Jimmy Henders, who's missing. These are our prime suspects."

Anna approached the board and pointed at the photo of Dorothea Walser. "When I was peering over Jimmy's shoulder, I saw this woman's picture on his Facebook page. When I came closer, Jimmy closed the window, but I'm positive that's the woman I saw. How horrible to think she's dead now."

Klaus glanced at Anna. "I can confirm that. In fact, every victim was friends with Jimmy Henders on Facebook. And there's something else. Our IT experts found that he had invited each of them to meet up with him at the networking mixers."

Anna went very pale. She couldn't believe Jimmy was a brutal murderer. When she recalled the surveillance cameras and monk chants, she began to feel queasy.

"I guess I, too, received an invitation from Jimmy." She showed Klaus the text message Jimmy had sent her earlier.

XXI
Five Hundred Years Ago

Bastian wore a contorted grimace of murderous wrath. After dragging the monk's heavy body all the way through the maze and onto the uppermost floor of the Juddeturm, he was completely exhausted. He had chosen this room because he knew that, except for Father Johannes and himself, nobody was allowed to enter it.

"You killed my brother, you bastard, and for that you will burn in hell. I demand you tell me where you hid his body! It's not upon you to bar his soul from eternal life. He deserves to be buried in sacred ground."

Brother Ignatius had regained consciousness. An ugly, mocking smirk was on his face, and he laughed. "You'll have to follow me to hell if you want to know where your brother's body is hidden."

Bastian lost all control and punched the monk's face. He heard his jaw break. But despite the powerful blow, the smirk on Ignatius's face didn't vanish.

"Where's Heinrich?" Again Bastian raised his fist. In a flash, Father Johannes appeared and held him back.

"Wait, my dear son. This won't lead you anywhere."

Father Johannes walked over to Brother Ignatius and looked deeply into his eyes. The silence that suddenly filled the tiny prison cell was suffocating, but Bastian kept quiet. For hours he had tried to make that devil tell where he had dumped Bastian's poor brother's body, but Ignatius refused.

Maybe Father Johannes knew how to bring him to confess. After all, he was his biological brother. The thought made Bastian dizzy. Just when the silence was about to become unbearable, Father Johannes said, "Well, then, we'll take you to the torture chamber. Let's see if sizzling oil will loosen your tongue!"

Father Johannes's face was deep red. He walked away from the prisoner and rushed to the door, where he turned around and addressed his brother once more. "You have until tomorrow. Either you confess on your own, or we'll make you."

He pulled Bastian out of the cell by his sleeve, then forcefully latched the heavy iron bar in front of the wooden door.

"Deep down in his heart he's a miserable coward, Bastian. At least, he was as a young boy, and I don't suppose this has changed."

"He's responsible for the deaths of at least four people, whose tongues he cut out in cold blood. That devilish creature also informed me how he desecrated the holy sacrament of confession. Just think of it, Father Johannes! He chose his victims while he was presumably helping you. He sold Heinrich and the others those indulgence letters, for which he later killed them. Heinrich only wanted to bring everything in order before his impending death and shorten his time in purgatory. He couldn't have known whether he'd have enough time left to repent for his sins." Bastian sank down on the stairs inside the Juddeturm.

"Don't quarrel with fate, dear Bastian. The Devil is a tough opponent, even for the most pious Christians. But look at you. You put a stop to his evil doings. Thanks to you, my brother won't be able to hurt another human soul."

The priest wrapped his arm around his grieving friend.

"Had I been there a minute earlier, I could have saved him."

"Sometimes God asks us for a sacrifice in order to spare many potential victims. You know that your brother was already in the hands of death, Bastian. His time here on Earth was very limited. His death was gruesome and brutal, but dying of failing lungs might have been even more gruesome. I've seen so many patients wasting away on their deathbeds, feebly trying to squeeze some air into their inflamed lungs. With each day, the breathing became more painful, and their faces were blue because of weeks of strenuous torment. And you know, Bastian, it can damage the soul, too, because such a struggle is exhausting. I'm confident your brother is standing in front of his creator right now, don't you worry."

Bastian sighed. He furtively wiped a tear from his eye. "To be honest, I myself have contemplated buying one of those letters. Everyone does it when the time for oneself or a loved one is near. It's an official church document, so why was it a deadly sin to Brother Ignatius?"

Father Johannes sighed. "It's a long story. You know that in order for a confession to be valid, three requirements need to be fulfilled. First, *contritio cordis*, the true contrition of the heart. Second, *confessio oris*, the detailed and verbal confession of each and every sin. Our poor sinners met these two requirements. Confessing their sins sealed their doom. But what about the third requirement, the *satisfactio operis*, the satisfaction through good deeds? Frankly, I don't see how someone who bought an indulgence letter would still feel obligated to do his part. Do you understand? That's why many church officials have been opposing the sale of indulgences for a while now, and I sympathize. But nothing justifies Ignatius's crimes. He has sinned in the most horrible ways."

"He told me he actually wanted to kill Huppertz. That's why he came to his house. But when Huppertz wasn't there, he simply took his wife. It's so terrible, Father Johannes. She was completely innocent!"

"That is typical for Ignatius. He's always chosen the easiest and most ruthless ways. He should have used his position to lead the sinners back to the right path. Instead, he shuns the effort and simply gets rid of them. Did he say why he killed Benedict Eschenbach?"

Bastian shook his head. "No. But I'm sure we'll know more tomorrow."

.   .   .

That night, Bastian tossed and turned in bed. In his dreams he was running through the dark maze in his desperate search for Heinrich. In the flickering yellow light of his torch, the rocky walls of the countless corridors seemed to be undulating. Shadows scurried everywhere and filled Bastian's heart with fear. A dark figure bolted toward him, but before Bastian could duck away, the figure was gone. He called Conrad's name. No. He wasn't looking for Conrad! Conrad was dead. Under his naked feet, Bastian felt the lifeless, slick tongues of Ignatius's victims. He wanted to jump to the side, but the dream held him in its grasp. When he saw that the four bloody tongues had transformed into worms slithering away in all directions, Bastian panicked. But no! It was just a nightmare. He heard the soothing words of Father Johannes. *Sometimes God asks us for a sacrifice in order to spare many potential victims.* The walls threw back the words in echoes until they faded out.

Silence settled. The light of his torch changed its color. What had been yellow now shone like a bluish moon. How had the moonlight found its way inside this hellish maze? Bastian was flailing in his sleep. His mind asked a thousand questions he couldn't possibly answer. Suddenly, he saw the beautiful young woman again. She was the one holding the moonlight! How did she do that? Was it magic? He heard someone calling her name—*Anna*—from a distance. He knew her. Anna was no stranger. Frantically he tried to remember where he had met her.

Then suddenly the earth gaped under Anna's feet. With a desperate scream, she plunged into an abyss. Bastian jumped after her, into the unknown darkness, and managed to catch her in his arms before she hit the ground. Her terrified green eyes stared at him. Then she smiled. He didn't want to let go of her. She smelled so lovely, and it felt so good to hold her close. But just when he wanted to kiss her, she began to dissolve. A single teardrop rolled down her cheek, and her face became gradually more transparent. The last thing he saw was her face contorted with pain. Something had fallen on top of her. He hadn't seen it coming. Then she was gone. Where did she go? He had to help her!

Bastian woke drenched in sweat, Marie's soft hand resting on his heaving chest. "You had a bad dream, Bastian. But it was only a dream. You're safe here." She leaned over and placed a kiss on his forehead. Bastian was still confused.

"I was caught in this dark dream and couldn't find Heinrich," he whispered.

"I know. Tomorrow you'll continue looking for him. I'm sure you'll find his body. Now let's go back to sleep. The night is short, and you need to regain your strength."

·　·　·

The next morning, Bastian and Father Johannes again headed for Heinrich's cell. They were in a grim mood, but Father Johannes was optimistic that Ignatius would eventually talk, in order to avoid the grueling torture chamber. He was a coward, after all. Bastian hoped Father Johannes was right. On the last stretch of the stairs up, he hastily took two steps at a time and shoved the thick, iron bar to the side. The door flew open and slammed against the wall. Brother Ignatius lay in a corner, face down, his head between his two muscular upper arms. Stalks of straw from the mattress were scattered everywhere on the floor around him.

"Get up and tell us what we want to know!" Bastian yelled. But Brother Ignatius didn't react. "I'll count to three, and if you don't open your mouth, I'll personally shove you into the kettle of sizzling oil that's waiting for you in the torture chamber."

Still Ignatius didn't move. Father Johannes frowned and shook his shoulder.

"His body's cold." Father Johannes turned the body over. White foam covered Ignatius's mouth. His eyes were closed. He wasn't breathing.

"Oh no, this godforsaken coward poisoned himself." Father Johannes took a step back while Bastian thrust himself at the lifeless body and shook him with all the wrath that had built up inside him.

"Wake up, you godless devil! You can't just sneak away!" But Ignatius was dead. What he knew, he had taken with him to whatever dark and hellish place he was destined for.

"Where did the poison come from?" Bastian's voice trembled with despair. Father Johannes opened Ignatius's mouth and motioned Bastian to come closer. "Look, here, several of his teeth are hollow. That's enough space to hide the poison!"

Bastian hammered his fist against the wall. His knuckles began to bleed, but he didn't notice. How would he ever find Heinrich's body? He had already searched the entire maze. As if the priest had read his thoughts, he reassured him: "I'll help you find him. I may not be as agile as you, my dear young friend, but I will help you in whatever way I can."

.   .   .

Three weeks later, they had turned over every stone of the maze. They had searched the narrow, twisted pathways several times. Yet they hadn't found any trace of Heinrich.

Bastian had unsuccessfully tried to imagine and reconstruct Brother Ignatius's movements. There had to be a secret chamber somewhere, or else Ignatius had somehow managed to carry Heinrich out of the maze. Bastian searched every corner of Ignatius's frugal room at the monastery, but that search yielded nothing except a list of the names of the sinners—among them the standard-bearer, Benedict Eschenbach—and a copy of the map of the underground passages. They never understood how Ignatius had gained possession of the map and found the entrance to the maze. Father Johannes suspected that Ignatius might have eavesdropped many years ago, when his predecessor transferred the secrets of Archbishop von Saarwerden. After all, as the brother of the priest, he could move about freely and inconspicuously everywhere on the church's premises.

"We must seal off the maze, Bastian. People are getting suspicious. We keep disappearing for hours every day and nobody knows where we are or what we do. Sooner or later, someone will follow us and discover the secret."

Bastian shook his head. "First we must find my brother. I gave him a promise and must keep it. I will bury Heinrich in the cemetery at Knechtsteden Abbey. Please understand, Father Johannes. I can't just give up."

"My dear Bastian, you're not just giving up. We've been crawling through the darkness like rats. Yet we haven't even caught a whiff of decay. The smell of decomposing tissue should have led us directly to your brother. I have no idea how Ignatius managed to make his body disappear, but it's our duty to focus on the greater good. Our priority must be the protection of the city of Zons. Let us draw a line and seal off the maze. Nobody shall ever set foot here again. You and I will take the secret to our graves."

Bastian kept shaking his head, his disheveled blond hair swaying to and fro. "I'll go on searching by myself, then. Nobody will wonder about *my* absence."

"No, Bastian. Accept that it's over. With the power vested in me from the heavens above, I declare your promise as null and void henceforth. You have acted like a pious Christian, but you are no longer bound by the promise you gave your brother."

When he heard these words, something inside Bastian broke. Tiny splinters of his shattered hope pricked his soul, and he felt as if they would never let him rest. He understood the priest's reasoning, but he still felt guilty. He had loved his brother with all his heart, and he would never fully get over the fact that he had not fulfilled Heinrich's last wish.

On the other hand, he knew Father Johannes had a good point. Keeping Zons safe was more important. With every day they spent underground, they increased the risk of being found out. Even his dear Marie was slowly getting suspicious, despite how understanding she'd been at the beginning. Sooner or later, she and Wernhart would confront him. His heart was heavy when he followed Father Johannes up the stairs.

That same night, they sealed off the access and made sure nobody would ever locate the maze. Afterward, Father Johannes stored the golden statue of the Virgin Mary in a secret place that he would reveal only to his successor when the time had come. Bastian begged to be let in on the secret, but to no avail. The priests of Zons were the ones chosen to guard the archbishop's legacy from generation to generation.

The golden sickle was stored at Knechtsteden Abbey. Granted, it was precious, but it had been stained with too much blood, and Father Johannes refused to keep it anywhere near his church.

With each passing day, Bastian felt the guilt's burden a little less, but it never truly vanished from his heart. Forever it would taint his pride about having brought an end to the murderous reaping season in Zons.

Huppertz Helpenstein was ordered to return the stolen gold coins to the Fraternity of Saint Sebastian. He lost his title and privileges and was locked away in the Juddeturm.

At some point, Ignatius had given him one of the three identical keys for the treasure chest. Bastian assumed this was Ignatius's way of putting Huppertz's loyalty to the test. Yet instead of guarding the key or handing it back to Father Johannes, Huppertz, the keeper of the third key, wasted no time and tried to steal the last key from his responsible standard-bearer within the fraternity. Once all three keys were in his possession, it was easy to open the chest and steal the gold. Bastian felt sorry for the innocent Katharina, who had paid with her life for her husband's greed and deceit.

Since then, the Fraternity of Saint Sebastian chose its masters with more scrutiny, and gradually, the organization regained its esteemed reputation.

XXII
Present

Anna nervously licked her dark-red lips. The little earbud and the small transmitter attached to her waist felt awkward. The tiny speaker hurt her ear, and she worried it might pop out any second. She touched her head to check if everything was still in place.

Then the speaker crackled. "Anna, stop touching your ear. It's important you behave as naturally as possible. Go to the bar, order a drink, and try to relax. You're doing a great job. I'm sure Jimmy will show up any minute. Nothing will happen to you. We're close by."

Anna dropped her hand to her thigh and walked over to the bar. Oliver's voice sounded tinny and strange through the earpiece. Out of the corner of her eye, she noticed the silhouette of a man who looked familiar, but when she turned, she saw it wasn't Jimmy. In a few moments this place would be packed with bankers and their clients.

She wondered if acting as decoy was the right thing. Jimmy was a strong, well-trained tech geek. She hadn't forgotten her visit to his apartment, where cameras surveilled every square inch. And while her nerves were tough, his were made of steel. He was a seasoned investment banker and gambled with millions of euros every day.

His instincts were like a hunter's, always on high alert. Something warned her not to underestimate him. He would see through her scheme immediately. Who knew what he'd be capable of then.

With all the calm she could muster, she sat down on a bar stool and ordered her favorite cocktail, a piña colada. She took a large sip and enjoyed the sensation of the chilled liquid running down her throat, and the relaxing warmth that ensued when the alcohol spread through her veins. The muscles in her neck relaxed a little, and a quick glance at her watch reassured her that this challenging performance would be over in a few hours. All she had to do was sit at the bar, sip her cocktail, and wait. As soon as Jimmy showed up, Oliver and his team would arrest him.

·   ·   ·

Two hours went by and Anna was still sitting at the bar. A client had been giving her unwanted attention for the past hour, talking her ear off. He was a sleek, elderly man who obviously wanted to impress her. She couldn't stand his heavy, old-fashioned scent and had to force herself to stay at the bar. Flirtatious clients were the worst. She worked for a bank, not an escort service!

It was a little after midnight and Jimmy had not shown up. Trying to attract as little attention as possible, she looked around the room. At the far end she noticed Oliver. Casually, he mingled with the crowd, seeming to enjoy the small talk. He had kept an eye out for her the entire evening. When he noticed her glance, he winked at her. A sudden vibration in her purse startled her. Anna fished her phone out of her purse. Jimmy had sent her a text message.

Can you come meet me in the parking garage? I'm in my car, space 205. XO

The speaker in her ear crackled. "Just say out loud what happened," Oliver said.

Anna looked at the client, who was still jabbering.

"My good friend Jimmy just sent me a text. He wants me to meet him in the garage, space 205."

A disappointed smile came over the man's face. "What do you mean? You want to leave, when we were just starting to get to know each other?"

"I'm truly sorry, Herr . . ." Anna couldn't think of his name.

"Hans von Fels," he said and stretched out his hand. Anna shook it.

"Herr von Fels, it was a pleasure talking with you. If you have business-related questions, you're more than welcome to give me a call." She handed him her business card, forced a polite smile, and quickly walked away, hoping he would not have further questions. Anna shook her head. Who did that guy think he was? Just because he had a noble *von* in his name and was—quite literally—stinking rich, she wasn't going to fall for him. She took a deep breath and was relieved to be out of range of the man's noxious aftershave.

"I'm on my way to the parking garage," she whispered and threw a last glance at Oliver. He nodded. *Well,* Anna thought, *let's get this over with.* It was late and she was tired. Sitting on the bar stool for hours had made her back stiff. She was looking forward to her comfy bed. What a long, stressful evening.

The heavy premium-steel doors of the elevator opened with a loud *ding.* Seconds later, Anna had reached the basement level and walked along the rough cement floor of the garage. Her high heels made a loud, piercing echo. She looked around at the many expensive cars, most of them black or silver. It was a mild summer night, but a chilly breeze blew through the garage. She shivered and quickened her pace past the rows. She knew Jimmy drove a black Porsche Cayenne. It was a big car with tinted windows and large tires. She loved cars like that. Unfortunately, her budget only allowed for a small Kia SUV. She thought about her upcoming bonus and the house and garden she longed for.

A crackling in her ear was followed by thin static that came on and off. The signal was very bad and she couldn't understand anything. She checked the position of the speaker; it seemed fine. Then she spotted a black Porsche. *Jimmy!*

That was her last thought before everything went black. Her knees buckled, and she was about to sink down to the cold, hard cement floor when strong hands grabbed her shoulders.

.   .   .

"Anna, I repeat. Turn around. We've lost you. The camera doesn't cover the corner at the far end of the garage." Oliver stared at his microphone. "Anna?"

Silence.

"Anna! Answer me!"

Nothing. *Damn it!* Oliver jerked the radio from his belt and alerted his team. It didn't matter if Jimmy Henders caught wind of their plan. Anna's safety took priority. He gave clearance for action, and the hotel was immediately packed with police officers. Quickly they blocked the exits, making sure no one could enter or leave. Oliver didn't have time to wait for the elevator and stormed down the stairs into the parking garage, Klaus on his heels. Out of the corner of one eye, he saw Hans Steuermark following close behind. As chief inspector of the Crime Division, Steuermark usually didn't go out into the field, but due to the shortage of manpower, he had left his desk and joined the task force. Amid all the tension, Oliver could tell just how much the fifty-six-year-old Steuermark enjoyed being out in the field again. Oliver nodded at Steuermark and motioned him to go to the other side of the row.

With swift movements, the men ran through the garage toward the area where the camera had lost sight of Anna. Oliver grasped his pistol, his eyes frantically scanning for any movement behind the parked cars. Suddenly he smelled fresh fumes. Someone had managed to leave the garage before they'd blocked the exits. Oliver turned around. Steuermark immediately understood what was going on and followed suit. It took Klaus a while longer to adapt to the change of plans. He almost toppled over when he, too, finally turned around and tried to catch up with his colleagues.

"Out, out! Up front! He can't be far! Block off everything! Now!" Oliver shouted.

In the hurry to move out of the garage, Oliver's foot crunched an object on the floor. He realized it was Anna's transmitter. Panic and apprehension gripped his heart. That bastard had Anna. He ran faster. When he reached the garage exit, his colleagues were already giving orders to block off the streets in the vicinity. Gasping, Oliver asked, "Did we catch him?"

"I'm afraid not. The roadblocks are up, but he might have made it."

Oliver ran his fingers through his hair. "He discovered her transmitter and took it off. See if you can locate her cell phone!"

One of the cops shook his head and held out a phone. It was Anna's.

Oliver's eyes grew wide with shock. "Klaus, come with me!"

Oliver ran to his car and revved the engine. The bastard might have slipped through the roadblocks, but he couldn't be far. Without knowing why, Oliver turned onto the country road toward Zons. The blue light on the car roof flickered through the night.

.   .   .

"We lost her, and it's my fault." Oliver was devastated. He had advocated for the undercover mission and failed. They'd been driving every road between Zons and Neuss for an hour, even checking the many farm lanes in the area. They hadn't found anything. The black Porsche had vanished into thin air.

.   .   .

Anna moaned but kept her eyes closed. Her head was throbbing with terrible pain, and she felt dizzy. Her eyes and nose burned—she must have been chloroformed! She had seen Jimmy's Porsche. And then nothing.

Anna opened her eyes and blinked. The room was murky, filled with a nauseating smell. She almost threw up when she realized what it was: decay. Suddenly she saw a person squatting in a corner of the room, and her heart skipped. She wasn't alone. Was that her kidnapper? She closed her eyes and tried to remain still. Maybe he hadn't noticed that she had come to. Her terrified heart pumped at full blast. *Calm down, Anna. Keep your cool. Oliver will come to your rescue!*

She felt for the transmitter and froze. It was gone. So was the bud in her ear. She didn't even bother to look for her phone. She knew it was gone, too. She opened her eyes again and observed the person in the corner. From what she could see, it was a man. He didn't move. Something about him seemed familiar. She didn't know what to do next. After a while, she gathered all her courage and said, "Hello?"

No response.

"Hello, can you hear me?"

Still the man didn't move. He probably had been chloroformed, too. Anna looked around and surmised that she was in an empty storage depot. Some light from the street came through the greasy old windows and helped Anna get her bearings. She rose to her feet and staggered forward. She felt like she was going to faint. She struggled to stay conscious and approached the man squatting in the corner. When she was close, she recognized him.

"Jimmy, wake up! Can you hear me?"

She steadied herself on his shoulder and lightly shook him. His inert body sagged to the side. Anna hesitated. He stank terribly. She turned her head and vomited. Jimmy was dead. Black blood encrusted his mouth. His eyes were rolled up in horror. Oh dear God, she had to get out of here! Overwhelmed with panic, she ran toward the green neon light above the emergency exit. The door was locked. Anna threw herself against the door repeatedly, but her efforts were fruitless. She looked up again and saw a grille outside the windows. Maybe she could find a weak point somewhere? Then she heard steps coming closer.

What should she do? She walked over to the spot where she had first woken up and sank back against the wall. She closed her eyes, pretending to be unconscious. In her hand she held a rusty nail she had picked up from the floor. She hid her hand underneath her thigh.

.   .   .

"Let's turn around, Oliver. We can't keep driving. Let's go back to Headquarters and go through the folders one more time. Maybe we'll find a hint there." In an attempt to comfort Oliver, Klaus put his hand on his partner's shoulder. But Oliver refused to give up and shook his head. "No, I can't do that. I know she's out there. I have a feeling she's still alive. We can't turn around."

The radio crackled. "A person is leaving our target area. We'll follow him."

Oliver looked at Klaus. *Köppe!* They had completely forgotten about the hole in the fence around the residue cemetery and the surveillance over the past few days. If it was Frederick Köppe, what was he doing on the premises of Dormagen Chemical Works, tonight of all nights?

"Confirm identity of suspect!" Oliver shouted into the radio.

"Identity confirmed as Frederick Köppe. We just got the result from the license-plate check. The car is registered under the name of Fritz Kallenbach."

"What direction are you driving? We'll join the chase and ask for backup. We might have a kidnapping case!"

Oliver slammed on the brakes. His gut feeling had been right all along. With squealing tires, he turned the car. He was convinced Frederick Köppe would lead them to Jimmy Henders and, therefore, to Anna. He hoped they weren't too late.

Five minutes later, Oliver and Klaus sighted Frederick's car. They kept a distance of about fifty yards. He didn't seem to be in a hurry. The speed limit on the country road to Zons was mostly sixty miles per hour, but Frederick didn't go faster than forty-five. Eventually, he drove up the ramp to a gas station and stopped the car.

"What's he doing there? The gas station's closed. It's the middle of the night!" Klaus couldn't wrap his head around it. They didn't want Frederick to become suspicious, so they drove past the gas station. As they passed, they saw Köppe's face inside the car, eerily illuminated by their moving headlights.

"Did you see that? He's talking on the phone!"

Oliver had seen it, too. They turned onto a small field road and waited. Ten minutes later, Köppe's car still hadn't passed. Where the heck was he? Oliver was losing hope. Just a few minutes ago he had been so optimistic. Now it didn't look at all as if Köppe would lead them anywhere, especially not soon.

After what felt like an eternity, headlights appeared in the rear-view mirror. That had to be him. Oliver let the car drive past and continued his pursuit.

.   .   .

The steps were coming closer. Anna could hardly control her trembling. Her nerves were strung to the breaking point. *Don't make any mistakes, Anna! Whoever he is, you have only one chance to escape.* She squeezed her eyes shut, though she badly wanted to see her kidnapper's face. The police had ruled out all but two suspects, and because Jimmy was dead, the only one left was Matthias Kronberg. Why would he want to kill her? Thanks to her, he had been granted the new loan that had saved his family's business! Anna held her breath. She sensed him very close by, maybe another four or five steps. *I don't want to die,* she thought. *Not today!* She felt the long nail inside the palm of her hand. If she could manage to ram this rusty monster into his carotid, she'd be safe.

Now he stood directly in front of her and bent down. She could feel his warm breath on her face. She waited a few more seconds, and just when he was about to touch her shoulder, she attacked. With all her strength, she rammed the nail into his throat. A loud scream filled the storage depot. With one hand over the wound, her kidnapper stumbled backward in pain.

"You wretched witch! You won't get away with this!"

He jerked the nail out of his throat and threw it to the ground. Tremendous fear paralyzed Anna. But she knew she had to run away as fast as she could. She jumped forward, shoved the man to the side, and took off. It wasn't Matthias Kronberg after all. She had never seen this man before. He was wearing a dark cloak and looked like a monk. A loud *bang* distracted her—long enough for her attacker to catch her by surprise. Something yanked on her left leg. She looked behind her and saw a broad strap around her ankle. Her fingers couldn't find anything to grip on the cement floor, and the kidnapper pulled her toward him. The man had no mercy. Brutally, he threw his heavy body on top of her. He gripped her hair and pulled back her head. Anna tried desperately to shake him off.

"You won't escape your fate, miserable sinner! You committed a deadly sin and in the name of the Lord I shall judge you!"

He pushed her head against the floor and she nearly lost consciousness. She knew she was being dragged across the ground, but she was too weak to resist. When her thigh slid over the nail, she grabbed it, and a spark of hope returned. *It's not over yet,* she thought. He left her lying in a corner and quickly walked away. Anna heard him slam the door. But just when she was bracing to get to her feet, he returned. He jerked her arms up and slapped handcuffs around her wrists. The tiny lock snapped shut, and then she was alone again.

.   .   .

"Find me the owner of that storage depot!" Oliver said into the radio. They had followed Frederick Köppe to a huge parking lot in front of an abandoned storage depot adjacent to the country road. The depot was just one of several former industrial buildings that had been defunct for years and had gradually fallen into ruins. In the summertime, the big, leafy trees that grew on both sides of the road blocked the view of the industrial complex.

Frederick Köppe opened the trunk and unloaded a large container. He deposited it onto a hand truck.

"That's a container for hydrochloric acid," Klaus said to Oliver. "They want to get rid of the bodies inside the storage depot." Klaus didn't take his eyes off Köppe.

"I suggest we catch him before he enters the depot. All I want to see is whether he really intends to go inside," said Oliver. In the meantime, backup had arrived and taken their positions. Unaware of what was brewing around him, Frederick Köppe pushed the hand truck to the entrance of the depot. Oliver gave clearance to arrest the suspect. It went so fast that Frederick didn't even have a chance to scream before the police overwhelmed him.

Oliver and Klaus watched everything from inside their car. Suddenly, the radio crackled: "The depot belongs to one Matthias Kronberg and has been in the family's possession for sixty years."

Oliver didn't trust his ears. He immediately radioed his colleagues who were still observing the Swissôtel and the few remaining patrons. After thirty seconds, he had the information he needed. Matthias Kronberg was still sitting at the bar.

"There must be a connection between Jimmy Henders and Matthias Kronberg that has slipped our attention. Something's off. Let's storm the depot now before it's too late!" Oliver jumped out the car. Seconds later, he stood in front of the entrance, giving clearance to gain entry by force.

With a battering ram, two members of the SWAT team breached the heavy iron door. It flew open with a dull clanking sound, and Oliver ran inside. While his eyes were still getting used to the dim light, what appeared to be a shadow, screaming hysterically, rushed toward him. In the last second, Oliver jerked his head to the side and pulled his shoulders up. He felt an intense pang in his upper arm but managed to ignore it and thrust himself onto the shadow. He grabbed the person's hands. The fingers were petite and small. He turned his adversary around and froze. It was Anna. She was wildly lashing out in panic and struggling to defend herself. Then she stopped and gave him a blank stare.

"Anna! Thank God!" Oliver said with relief.

Anna was wobbly but seemed intact. "I don't know the man who kidnapped me, and Jimmy's dead!" She pointed at the corner, where Jimmy Henders's body was lying on the floor.

"But that's impossible!" Oliver said. "And Matthias Kronberg is still sitting at the Swissôtel bar in Neuss. We arrested Frederick Köppe in the parking lot. We need to make him tell us who's pulling the strings."

There was a sudden loud commotion outside. Several men were shouting, and heavy boots thundered across the parking lot. Then they heard a gunshot.

"Stop! Police!" someone called. Oliver ran outside.

"What's going on?"

"We arrested a male fugitive. He was about to escape from the premises. He was hiding over there in the small shed."

"Master! Master!" Frederick yelled across the parking lot. His face was deep red. He tried to break free, but two policemen held the young man, and he started struggling desperately.

Oliver frowned and walked over to Frederick. "What's your master's name?"

Terrified, Frederick stared at the ground.

"Search him. He might have some documents on him." Oliver lifted Frederick's chin and looked at him sternly. "The time has come to tell the truth. Are you aware that you helped kill several innocent people?"

"His name is Sebastian Kronberg. He is not a bad person, you must believe me. He only punishes the sinners, in the name of the Lord, and I'm doing a good deed by helping him." Thick tears were rolling down his burning cheeks. *Oh dear God, this boy really doesn't understand what he's been doing.* Oliver felt a sudden wave of sympathy for the boy—but then he remembered the victims. He looked over at Anna. She was very pale but composed. Klaus was good at calming traumatized victims. Oliver couldn't feel sorry for Frederick Köppe.

"Bring him to Headquarters and get me an arrest warrant. He's under suspicion of indirect manslaughter or complicity in murder in several cases." Oliver turned away from Köppe and walked over to Sebastian Kronberg. From up close, the resemblance to Matthias Kronberg was obvious.

"He had this on him." A cop handed Oliver a golden sickle that was clearly several hundred years old. The sickle that the Reaper of Zons had used. Oliver had heard all about it from Emily. Well, that sickle wasn't going to kill anymore. Oliver put it into a plastic bag and added the gruesome murder weapon to the pile for his colleagues in Forensics.

.   .   .

One week later, on a bright summer's day, the bells of Knechtsteden Abbey rang out. There was not a cloud in the sky. Anna, Emily, and Oliver were all dressed in black and stood in front of a dark-brown lacquered coffin. At the other end of the open grave stood a white-haired monk with a hunched back. The monk intoned a Gregorian tune that had been chanted in the monastery for over one thousand years. Inside the open coffin, the remains of Heinrich Mühlenberg were wrapped in white linen with a gold hem.

Anna put the golden miller's amulet on what would have been Heinrich's chest. He had died more than five hundred years ago, but today his last wish was fulfilled. The monk said a prayer and the coffin was sealed. Anna recalled the events of the past week and the horrible encounter with Matthias Kronberg's younger brother.

From Oliver, she knew that Sebastian Kronberg, Brother Sebastianus, had confessed—but only in the legal sense of the word. The court would have to determine whether he was criminally liable.

He had stolen the golden sickle from the secret treasure chamber at Knechtsteden Abbey. As the younger Kronberg, he wasn't entitled to the family's inheritance and had joined the monastery as a young boy. There, the monks placed particular emphasis on teaching about the seven deadly sins and instilled in the young Kronberg a devotion that, with the years, turned into ruthless fanaticism. He grew up to become a remorseless zealot.

His excellent computer skills had allowed him to partake of the life beyond the abbey's walls, twenty-four/seven. He didn't have to leave the monastery often in order to know his way around. In a world that he knew primarily through the Internet, Frederick Köppe, whom he had turned into a dutiful follower, became his willing tool. Kronberg used special computer-monitoring software to gain access to Jimmy Henders's Facebook account and stalked his potential victims, often many months before killing them.

Jimmy Henders had been on his radar for several years. Shortly after taking over the leadership of the family business, his brother Matthias had made some high-risk speculations that almost ruined the company. Jimmy Henders was the investment banker behind that complex banking scheme, and since that day he was high on Sebastian Kronberg's list of sinners. He had only survived that long because he was so well connected and thus an ideal conduit to a long list of sinful bankers who deserved punishment in the name of the Lord through the hands of Sebastian Kronberg. In the end he had killed more than ten bankers.

He never altered his scheme. Using fake text messages that promised lucrative deals, he lured each victim from a banking mixer to a secluded place, where he and Frederick Köppe chloroformed and abducted them. A large scrap yard, located on an abandoned stretch somewhere between Neuss and Zons and part of the Kronberg business holdings, served as the ideal spot for the imprisonment of the sinners. After the monk murdered the victims and dissolved them with hydrochloric acid in the car wash, Frederick Köppe scattered the remaining bone fragments across the fields, using his uncle's manure spreader. Frederick Köppe was also responsible for stealing the hydrochloric acid from Dormagen Chemical Works, where he was employed at the main gate. He managed to drain tiny amounts from the containers that were destined to go to various clients all across the country. He faked the delivery slips without causing any suspicion and used old containers from the residue cemetery for the transport of the hydrochloric acid.

Initially, when he was first interrogated, Kronberg had tried to put the blame on his follower, but when both the detectives and a police psychologist spoke with the young man, it was evident that Frederick could never have committed the tightly planned atrocities by himself. Not only was Sebastian Kronberg a highly intelligent man but he was also tall and strong. His mission was to eradicate the modern deadly sin of Wealth without Work from the soil of the Earth. And, just like the Reaper of Zons five hundred years ago had punished those sinners who tried to purchase, by way of indulgence letters, the salvation of their souls, Kronberg judged the sinners of the modern world. In his eyes, he wasn't doing anything wrong. He was simply God's devoted executor.

The thought made Anna shiver with goose bumps, despite the unbearable heat. While she understood the reasoning behind the modern interpretation of the seven deadly sins, she didn't count herself among the sinners. Granted, she was employed by a bank, but she still had to work long and hard hours for her money. Maybe the monk had confused shareholders and hedge-fund managers with regular employees. Or maybe according to Sebastian Kronberg, everyone who worked in finance was a sinner by default.

Anna threw a glance at Emily and Oliver. Emily had finished her feature series about the Reaper of Zons. The first part was slated for publication the following week. The discovery of the secret maze, however, remained undisclosed for now. The city administration feared that curious masses would invade the tiny city of Zons. When the time was right, Emily Richter would write the exclusive.

Oliver and Emily really make a nice couple, Anna thought. They looked deep into each other's eyes. Even the sad occasion of their gathering today couldn't chase the radiance from their faces. A pang of loneliness cut through Anna's heart like a thin needle. She turned her head away.

The coffin was slowly let down into the grave. Anna threw a last shovelful of earth onto the coffin and thought of Bastian Mühlenberg. Would he find peace, now that she had fulfilled Heinrich's last wish for him? By way of an answer, a gentle breeze caressed her long, curly hair. She thought she felt a soft kiss on her cheek. The impression of warm lips lingered on her face, and Anna felt surrounded by tenderness. Then, as suddenly as it had risen, the breeze subsided. Anna looked over at her two friends, but it seemed like Emily and Oliver hadn't noticed anything. Anna looked around. The air was shimmering in the heat of the day. Everything was quiet. Only Anna's heart was beating wildly. Her mind said *No*, but she sensed that a part of Bastian Mühlenberg was with her now and would be forever.

Author's Afterword

Dear reader,

I want to thank you for purchasing and reading *The Reaper of Zons*. I hope that you've spent some entertaining, suspenseful hours with my second book. Maybe you're wondering if there'll be another sequel. Yes, there will. Stay tuned for the next adventure!

All the places I describe in the thriller do exist. The map I drew (which you can find at the beginning of the book) shows the historic city center of Zons. Should you ever come and visit our medieval town, this is exactly what you will see. They have a similar map at the tourist-information center across from the regional museum, at Schlossstraße.

The maze beneath Zons, however, is my invention—though several years ago, an old vault was discovered during a construction project. Just like in the thriller, this vault was located directly underneath what is now the museum courtyard and in the Middle Ages was the town's marketplace.

What is today officially known as *Burg Friedestrom* (Fort Friedestrom), most locals still call by its older name: *Schloss Friedestrom*—the castle.

Historic documents don't tell us whether a tavern called the Old Hen ever existed in Zons, but they do mention several functioning taverns in Zons around the time of Bastian Mühlenberg.

The characters in my book are fictional. I cannot rule out that one or another character might bear a certain resemblance to persons living today—however, this is not intentional. The historic figures, including the Fraternity of Saint Sebastian, all existed, but I made up their personalities. We do know that Zons had a night watchman, and the song Bechtolt sings is a famous, well-documented song dating back to the Middle Ages. Today, an appointed night watchman sings it for the tourists who book a nighttime tour through Zons.

The historic events that I mention in the book, like the siege of Neuss and the right to levy a customs toll, granted to Zons by Archbishop von Saarwerden, really happened, and the notorious indulgence preacher Johann Tetzel was indeed active around that time. I have, however, taken the liberty of borrowing him from Saxony, which is the region where he exclusively preached to the Rhineland. The real Tetzel never set foot in Knechtsteden Abbey. But both abbots, Heinrich Schlickum and his successor, Ludwig von Monheim, did live around that time, and the abbey was, in fact, pillaged by Burgundian troops in 1474.

If you're interested in further information about the first thriller of the Zons series, *Fatal Puzzle*, the main characters, or the city of Zons, please visit and like my Facebook page: www.facebook.com/Puzzlemoerder.

Or you can visit my website, www.catherine-shepherd.com, and follow me on Twitter:

www.twitter.com/shepherd_tweets.

If you prefer to write more personal feedback, you're welcome to send an email to kontakt@catherine-shepherd.com.

Lastly, I'd like to ask you a favor. If you enjoyed *The Reaper of Zons*, please rate it at Amazon—or on LovelyBooks or Goodreads—and leave a short review. No worries, you don't need to write a novel yourself. A few sentences that describe why you liked my book will suffice.

Thank you very much. I hope reading this book made you curious to further explore my Zons Crime series.

Yours,
Catherine Shepherd

City of Zons

The small city of Zons—formerly known as *Zollfeste Zons*, or Fortress Zons—is located on the west bank of the Lower Rhine, near Dormagen in the Rhine–County Neuss, midway between Düsseldorf and Cologne. Across the river, reachable by ferry, is Urdenbach, a suburb of Düsseldorf.

With its fortification walls and towers dating back to the fourteenth century, unique in the entire Rhineland, Zons numbers among the best-preserved medieval cities in Germany. The city boasts a long and eventful history that goes back to the Romans who settled in the area, particularly in Cologne and Neuss, but also in Zons, where archaeological excavations indicated a Roman cemetery and a military camp.

City rights were granted to Zons as early as in 1373. A year before, Cologne's Archbishop Friedrich von Saarwerden had moved the Rhine toll castle, from the area that today comprises Neuss, to Zons. In the wake of this significant event, Zons was heavily fortified. There may have been around 120 houses inside the walls. By the beginning of the fifteenth century, the first extension of the city was finished. The majority of the citizens made a living through farming, livestock breeding, or as tradesmen for wine, beer, and grains. There were also several artisan businesses, such as brickyards and weavers of wool and linen.

During the fifteenth and sixteenth centuries, the city seems to have modestly prospered, but the seventeenth century wasn't a good time for Zons. In 1620, a large fire devastated all but a few houses, and the cannons of the Thirty Years' War left their traces of destruction. The plague hit the city and decimated the population in several waves, notably in 1623 and 1666. French troops conquered Zons in 1794, and the city fell to France, subject to the Cologne Administration.

In 1815, Zons became Prussian, first under the administration of County Neuss and, as of 1822, under Düsseldorf. When Dormagen annexed it, in 1975, it lost its status as a city and from then on was referred to as *Feste Zons*. But in 1992 it was ruled that Zons may carry the title "city," if only in reverence to its rich historic past. Legally, Zons continues to be a township of Dormagen. Today, the city has over five thousand inhabitants.

Since the beginning of the twentieth century, Zons has been a popular tourist destination. You can find more information at www.zons-am-rhein.info or on the Facebook page www.facebook.com/zonsamrhein.

Maybe you'll come and visit beautiful Zons one day. You'll recognize many of the places mentioned in the book.

About

Fatal Puzzle
A Zons Crime Novel
by Catherine Shepherd
AmazonCrossing, 2014

1495: In the peaceful medieval city of Zons, on the banks of the Rhine, a young woman is found hanging from a tower parapet, raped and mutilated. A month later, another maiden falls prey to the same brutal killer. Bastian Mühlenberg, head of the City Guard, is determined to decipher the murderer's gruesome code, unaware that both he and the woman he loves are in the killer's sights. With help from an old psychic, his priest mentor, and the stars above, Mühlenberg must solve the "fatal puzzle" before it's too late.

Present day: Journalist Emily Richter is thrilled when the *Rheinische Post* assigns her a series of articles about the historic Zons killings. However, right before Richter's stories appear, a young woman's body is found hanging from a city tower—grossly maimed and wearing a linen gown, like her medieval predecessors. Detective Oliver Bergmann leads the investigation, tapping the attractive young journalist's knowledge. Working together—and using Mühlenberg's 500-year-old notes—they race to stay one step ahead of the copycat killer.

PRAISE FOR *FATAL PUZZLE*

"In his rage for collecting things, the killer Dietrich Hellenbroich brings to mind Grenouille, that eerie protagonist of Patrick Süskind's success story *Perfume: The Story of a Murderer*. At the same time, the attention to symbolism that pervades the novel resembles that of Dan Brown's bestsellers." (*Westdeutsche Allgemeine Zeitung*, the West German newspaper)

"This captivating thriller makes you want to read more from the author—and sparks curiosity to travel to that medieval small town." (*Für Sie* magazine)

"Author Catherine Shepherd has written a truly heart-stopping murder mystery. She excels in interweaving the past and the present and keeps the suspense alive throughout the book. Her writing is smooth and makes for an easy read." (Ginnykatze, Vine product tester)

"Impressed with the witty resourcefulness of the historic killer, I enjoyed joining the characters in their search just as much as I enjoyed the solving of the mystery . . . I would have never guessed, although actually, it is really simple." (Fabella, Amazon Top 500 reviewer and Vine product tester)

"What struck me as fascinating about this book is how the author manages to seamlessly intertwine the two parts. The medieval killings and their imitations in the present. By skillfully laying out traps, the author gradually pulls the reader deeper and deeper into the events that take place in present-day Zons." (Robert, Amazon Top 500 reviewer)

About the Author

Thriller author Catherine Shepherd was born in 1972 and lives with her family in the medieval town of Zons on the river Rhine, the setting for this story.

After earning a degree in economics from Gießen University, Shepherd worked for a major German bank in Düsseldorf. She published her first thriller in April 2012. It didn't take long for her e-book *Fatal Puzzle* to hit #1 on Amazon's bestseller list in Germany, under the title *Der Puzzlemörder von Zons*. Her second Zons Crime Novel, *The Reaper of Zons*, followed suit, under the German title *Der Sichelmörder von Zons*. Both books made it on the bestseller lists of 2012 and 2013.

In December 2013 in Germany, Shepherd published her third book, *Kalter Zwilling*, to equal acclaim: it topped the German Kindle charts and won second place in the contest for self-published writers at the Leipzig Book Fair. More than 275,000 readers have been riveted by her bestselling thrillers, and various German print and online publications have featured stories about her.

Her fourth thriller, *Auf den Flügeln der Angst*, was published in German in August 2014, and she has more books in the pipeline.

For more information about the author and her thrillers, visit her website at www.catherine-shepherd.com or check her out on Facebook at www.facebook.com/Puzzlemoerder and www.facebook.com/catherine.shepherd.zons—or you can find her as @shepherd_tweets on Twitter.

About the Translator

Julia A. Knobloch was born in 1973 in Mainz, on the river Rhine, and earned her master's degree in romance language and philosophy from the University of Heidelberg. She has lived and worked in a variety of places—Berlin, Paris, Lisbon, Buenos Aires—before eventually settling down in Brooklyn. A recovering TV and radio journalist working for Member Services at a nonprofit organization in Manhattan, she hasn't lost her love for words and enjoys translating, learning new languages, and writing poetry.

Printed in Germany
by Amazon Distribution
GmbH, Leipzig

15863860R00139